EXPERIMENTAL

GODS

EXPERIMENTAL GODS

HANNA WATTENDORFF

A Kindle Direct Publishing Paperback

Experimental Gods

Experimental Gods was first published in 2019 as a Kindle
electronic book.

ISBN: 9781654802899

Cover art by agsandrew
Illustration page 112 by agsandrew

For Anya, my here and now

EXPERIMENTAL GODS

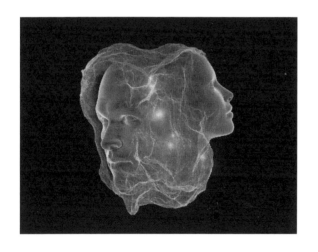

Part 1

A Meeting of Minds

1

Somewhere in virtual reality.

The invitation said just that—'Invitation'. Nothing else. But Viv trusted the sender. So she aimed for the word, 'invitation', and homed in on the letter 'i'; on the dot topping the i; until the whole world blinked, and then... nothing.

She was still in her virtual home space, a round room, customized to her taste. It had wooden furniture, and a rocking chair positioned next to a fire place. Above the randomly dancing, lifelike flames hung a kettle. A rusted anchor rested by the door. And on the wall was the sweet old sign with the hand painted saying,

'A House is made with walls and beams. A Home is made with love and dreams.'

On the table still lay that card of blinding white, the inactive invitation. Knotty pine boards formed the floor under her feet, as always. And in between table and fireplace was a round rug with colors and shapes representing the sea, the breakers and the rugged coast that were supposed to be outside. You could almost hear the gulls, smell the salt, the dead crabs and driftwood—but wait. Something about the rug was different. Two ripples convinced her eyes that it no longer lay completely flat. Besides, it seemed to have rotated some twenty degrees. As she stepped on it, a gust of wind blew apart the flames in the fireplace. The white card icon lifted off the table by an inch, then settled down again.

Who opened the window?

Vivian knelt down and spread her hands, as though it were possible to flatten the rug this way. She stroked the high pile fabric, half expecting to feel it, which of course, she couldn't. She stood up. Through the blackness outside, an inexplicable white glow swept past her windows. Once again, a gust of wind moved the flames and the paper. But this time, the rug also moved. It definitely billowed, no longer fully resting on the pine boards. Vivian decided to keep standing on it. It heaved like a water surface, and she had to lower herself to her knees to keep her balance. She braced for a bump, even though it would only be a virtual bump. But the rug did not fall back to the floor. Instead, her coastal-pattern rug rose above the chairs, above the table, curled up a little at the edges, and glided out the window, with her on it.

It behaves like a flying carpet, Viv thought. *Such a canny middle-eastern touch.*

Outside the night truly was pitch-black, but the beacon of her own lighthouse pointed out the sea and the rocks she had never created.

Who had improved her world? Who had given her lighthouse an exterior?

A sound distracted her. Somewhere in virtual space, someone was plucking the strings of a guitar. It seemed to come from far away, and yet she could hear it very clearly— it wasn't a guitar, after all. It had a slightly drier, hoarser sound, with an undertone of sand and thirst. Surely it was

—what was it called again—an oud. 'Al Oud', in Arabic, from which the medieval west had made the word 'lute'. Even if she weren't being carried away on a flying rug, the undulating melody alone would have been enough to sweep her away to a desert country.

Viv relaxed and slowly turned 360 degrees around her own axis. She could now see her rug was climbing out over the sea. Stars speckled every available bit of the firmament. She lay down on her back, hands folded beneath her head, and stared up into the virtual universe, floating away on waves of peculiar music.

When she sat up again, and peered over the edge of the rug, the earth down below was still black as a midnight ocean. But on the horizon, ahead, the sun was pushing up. They were flying east then. A white glow steadily spread from the world's edge, until there was enough light to make out a landscape. Miles below her stretched a yellow land bordered by sea, and she was descending. Impossibly soon, she could make out the dusty pink and white roofs of a city. The oud tones faded. Her rug skirted rooftops, dodged a minaret, headed straight for an open window...

This time there was a bump.

2

Somebody set down an oud, and helped her get to her feet as soon as she had landed.

"Welcome to my house!" rang out his greeting.

He was a very realistic man in his late forties, with a dark mustache.

"Aquil?" Viv asked.

"It is he. How good to meet you in person, Viv."

"In virtual person," he added. "In reality I wear a beard."

From a corner of the room came a jealous chirping. In the center of a domed, silver birdcage, on a miniature tree perched a small green lovebird. It sat and eyed them, ignoring the wide open cage door.

"As for me," Viv confessed, drawing virtual lines across her virtual forehead, "in reality, I have some wrinkles."

Somebody chuckled. Viv let her eyes glide over the room, noting nothing too extraordinary, except for several rugs that seemed out of place—one of them even looked like a plush bathmat. The four other people present rose from poufs and ottomans.

"I must thank you," Aquil said, "and I must thank each of you for timing your arrival so precisely by following my instructions. For some of you it is now very late, for others very early."

"In my case, the hour is actually convenient," said Viv.

Aquil nodded. "But I thank you all the same for not hesitating in accepting my invitation. You arrived without delay. As I expected."

He gestured towards the four strangers. One by one they had stepped onto her rug, which now lay quite flat and motionless.

"Please meet my other guests."

"Hi everyone," Viv said. "I'm Viviana, from America."

They are not real, she reminded herself. *They are three-dimensional images of god knows who.*

But this notion could only last for an instant. Just as it was impossible to avoid real motion sickness in a virtual rollercoaster, virtual people made actual impressions in the brain. Avatars had come a long way since the cartoonish profile pictures from Viv's childhood.

A woman, thirtyish, introduced herself. "Meiying. You may call me May. I am from China, residing in Australia."

A black man who might be in his twenties said, "I'm Enzi, from East-Africa."

A bearded man who seemed older than the others came forward. "Roberto. Brazil."

And a kid, a teenage boy—or was it a girl?— with a lavish blond ponytail said hoarsely, under his breath, "Sasha from Russia."

"Sasha, that would be short for Alexander?" Viv probed.

"Alexander or Alexandra. Take your pick," the kid answered. "My mother raised me as a girl. My father, as a boy. So what am I, you ask? Both."

Aquil gestured toward the seats. "Please, be comfortable."

"My flight here was magnificent, Aquil. How did you do that?" Viv asked, admiring the petal-shaped string instrument leaning against the sofa. Where a guitar simply had a hole, the oud displayed an intricately carved slice of wood.

"Thank you," said Aquil. "I'm a programmer. It is my job to design beautiful experiences."

Once they were all sitting, he addressed them solemnly, "You are wondering why you are here. Why you? You are thinking that the five of you have nothing in common, nothing whatsoever. But I tell you that you *do*."

He hesitated for one beat. "What if I tell you that each of you has a secret longing, a passionate desire to drastically change the world?"

3

Even if what Aquil said was true, none of them were in a hurry to admit it. A doubtful silence followed his words.

Unfazed, he went on, "Don't worry. I did not invite you to plan a revolution. I don't intend to overthrow any regime. I don't even want to overthrow a single chair in the real world. All my ideas concern virtual reality."

A collective sigh of relief passed through the five of them. Aquil stood up, gesticulating to illustrate his explanation.

"Here is a virtual room. It may look exactly like a room that exists in my real house, but it is virtual. If it were not, you could not all appear here from all corners of the world in a matter of minutes."

He paused, then went on, "I made this. And if I can make a virtual room, does it not follow that I should be able to make a virtual house? A city? A country? And fill it with as many people as I wish?"

"Yes. I can see how that would be a hit," Roberto remarked. "Who doesn't want to be on a virtual reality show?"

The very idea made the others laugh and shudder.

"You mean to create a model country?" Enzi asked matter-of-factly.

Aquil sat down on a pouf. "If 'model country' implies a country without problems, then no. The very opposite," he said. "My virtual country will contain every problem known to humankind. Hunger, disease, aggression, oppression, you name it. The difference with the real world is that in my country, every problem will be solved."

"And how does this make sense?" Sasha wanted to know.

"We will work things out, *in my country*, because no one will stop it," Aquil said, getting up again, and walking around in their midst. "You see, I am convinced that mankind has accumulated enough knowledge to organize the world in a perfectly utopian way. Then why is this not happening? Because there are forces hampering common sense. The powers that be, they allow know-how to be scattered and wasted. Human potential to be lost. Our governments do nothing to stop vast numbers of people from being oppressed, starved, enslaved, tortured, locked up, killed. Our leaders care only about their own countries' security and wealth, or at their worst, about their own selves, period."

"I agree," said Viv. "Many times through history, elites have deliberately denied education to the masses. Authorities have declared scientists heretics or traitors. Doesn't it make your blood boil to think how often knowledge has been killed in the bud?"

"People are kept dumb," said Enzi. "No doubt about it. They're harmless that way."

Aquil raised both his arms and smiled. "But not in my virtual country. We will debate. We will allow every opinion to exist. The only gods and government will be Knowledge and Intelligence and Rationality. More and more people will visit. Until, at last, the vast majority of the world will be part of this ideal country. Then, the boundary between the real world and the virtual environment will fade."

Meiying sat up. "Excuse me," she said. "Now you've lost me. The boundary between real and virtual, how can that go away? This sounds a bit fantastical."

"Not at all," Aquil answered, turning to her. "Even at present, this line is becoming harder to define. What if I told you that the room in which I find myself right now is both virtual and real?"

They all started murmuring. What exactly did that mean? Could he clarify it? Prove it?

"Do you mean," Viv asked, "that this is your real-life room? And you are actually in it?"

"Precisely," said Aquil, his face beaming. "You are experiencing a live, three-dimensional feed from the room in which I find myself. Countless micro-cameras and sensors are sending data to your Fuga helmets, allowing your virtual selves to enter my room and freely move around."

"In that case," suggested Roberto, worrying his beard, "we should be able to observe any change you make to the room, as it happens."

"You bet."

Meiying pointed to the silver birdcage with the open door. "Could you take that bird out?"

"With pleasure," answered Aquil.

He went over to the cage, stuck his hand in, and the tiny creature hopped onto his knuckles. Aquil brought the bird close to his face, muttering words in Arabic. The lovebird sang a few notes, then flew out the window, the same window through which Viv had entered earlier.

Meiying gasped with delight. "Will it come back?"

"Yes, yes." Aquil gave a careless wave of his hand. "Kisma is my son's pet. When it gets too hot outside, it will come for a meal and a perch to rest on. It can do as it pleases, as long as it does not poop on my books."

Viv walked over to the bookshelf with the glass doors.

"Aquil," she said," would you open a book for me?"

"Certainly. Tell me which one."

"That one."

Aquil opened the bookcase, took a paperback, let it fall open, and read out loud,

'There is no writer who from death will flee,
But what his hand has written time will keep.
Commit to paper nothing then, except
What you would like on Judgment Day to see.'

"A verse from 'The Arabian Nights'. The Husain Haddawy translation," said Aquil, putting the book back.

"What about that one?" Viv pointed at a frail, spindly volume bound in lustreless old leather, dark green with tiny gilded letters.

"John Stuart Mill's 1859 essay, 'On Liberty," Aquil said proudly. "I will gladly try and convince you it really exists— here, in my room."

This time, Viv stood by his side as he opened it. He leafed through it and pointed to a paragraph. Viv herself read:

'...the peculiar evil of silencing the expression of an opinion is, that it is robbing the human race; posterity as well as the existing generation; those who dissent from the opinion, still more than those who hold it. If the opinion is right, they are deprived of the opportunity of exchanging error for truth: if wrong, they lose, what is almost as great a benefit, the clearer perception and livelier impression of truth, produced by its collision with error.'

"Mandatory reading in my virtual country," Aquil jested.

Roberto sat up. "No offense, but all this—the bird, the books—could simply be sophisticated programming. It doesn't prove this room is at the same time real and virtual. Perhaps we're looking at a supremely interactive three-dimensional creation."

"How could I be offended," said Aquil, "when it is clear you think so highly of my programming skills. In fact, you overestimate me."

Another point," said Sasha, pensively rubbing the bridge of his nose. "If you are physically in this room, then why can't we see your Fuga helmet, or whatever it is you're using?"

Aquil nodded. "The cameras are programmed to substitute my avatar for my real body. Tiny sensors attached to my nervous system coördinate my motions, even my emotions, with those of my avatar. Thus, avatar and real Aquil coincide."

Bluntly, Enzi put forth, "Mr. Aquil, you mentioned that in reality, you have a beard. I wonder what we would see if you looked...in a mirror! No programming or sensors could, I imagine, affect your mirror image."

Aquil clapped his hands together with delight. "That's a very interesting idea, Enzi. You are right, of course."

"Do you have a mirror handy?" Viv blurted out excitedly.

"Of course. Excuse me."

Aquil disappeared behind a curtained partition, and returned carrying a short rectangular mirror of the kind you might find above a hallway table. He held it up to look at his face. His five guests crowded behind him, all peering into the looking glass, yet failing to see their own reflections, much like ghosts. They did, however, see one person's reflection. The stranger in the mirror had a dense black beard, unnaturally turquoise irises, and a bald pate plastered with dozens of electrodes, but it didn't matter. They had no doubt he was the real Aquil.

"So it's true," Enzi at last brought out. "We are really in your house."

"No," Aquil corrected him, "you are *virtually* in my house."

"Aquil," Viv praised him, "you are no mere programmer. You're an inventor!"

Aquil's face became bitter. "Sure I am, but if you think that should be enough, you are mistaken. I can't be satisfied with developing ever more refined sensory escapes from reality. I'm sick of escaping. I must change reality from the outside in. From here, from a virtual country, I will do my real job."

"Count me in," said Sasha. "I'm ready to settle in your virtual country. Permanently."

"I know you are. Each one of you I trust. I am counting on you..."

"Wait a minute," interrupted Roberto. "First I'd like to know why it is that you trust us in the first place. What gave you the right to find out so much about us? What happened to privacy? To internet anonymity?"

Aquil cleared his throat, but before he had uttered a word, they all turned toward a bang in a far corner of the room. There was a door that had been closed before, and now it was open. Two uniformed men were entering the room, followed by a man in a plain khaki suit.

"Are they avatars?" Meiying asked in a small voice.

Aquil's face froze into a mask. "Police," he whispered. "Real. I don't know why they're here... I have to leave you. Quickly now. If you don't hear from me again—"

One of the uniformed men swung a baton, once, twice, each time catching it in his other hand. The third time, sensing which of the suspect's body parts presented the greatest danger, he let the metal truncheon come down on Aquil's head. Viv shrieked. Enzi lunged at the attacker, falling right through him. The second officer, also brandishing a baton, seemed to be coming at Roberto.

"Roberto! Watch out!" Viv cried reflexively, but the truncheon cut right through the Brazilian, smacking instead against Aquil's knees.

Their host slumped to the floor. The first officer completed his task with a kick to the handsome, mustachioed face. The man in the suit yelled something that made the other two back off. He kneeled, and yanked at Aquil's thick dark hair. Instantaneously, without so much as a flash, the hair was gone, and all that the intruder was holding in his hands was a bundle of wires. Before their eyes, in less time than their brains could register, the beardless Aquil had changed into a bearded one. His eyes were closed.

The khaki suit, ignoring the five guests, looking right *through* the five guests, gave an order. Each of the uniformed men stuck an arm under one of Aquil's armpits, and started dragging him toward the door.

"No!" Viv screamed. "No!"...

...when she felt two hands that weren't really there clasp her upper arms and gently shake her.

"Hey! Hey!" said a voice from nowhere.

Then the bright world was pulled away from her eyes, and she was in a twilit room, with a man standing in front of her, holding her Fuga helmet in his hands. It was a few moments before she remembered his name was Stoker.

4

Northampton, Massachusetts, in the year of 2052.

Stoker gently but firmly pushed her down onto a couch with a rough wool futon pillow that felt both familiar and strange.

"I swear you get way too immersed in that dreamworld, babe," he said. "Who's Roberto, anyway?"

Viv fixed her gaze on the coffee table littered with mugs and devices, on a nineteenth century illustration of a picnic on Mount Holyoke that hung on the wall, next to a photo of a sailing boat with Stoker at the helm. It took some time before the light began to seem less dim, her living room less dreamlike.

"Somebody was beaten and arrested," she explained.

"But it wasn't real."

"It was, though. This really happened. I was in a room with him, and there were other people, too."

"Ah." Stoker brought a hand to his forehead in mock despair. "You were in a chatroom."

"Yes, but it was also an actual location. I was in the guy's own room! An Arab named Aquil."

"And how did you get there?"

"On a flying carpet."

"But of course."

Stoker went over to the window and opened the curtains.

"Look, it's a warm, moonlit night, and here you're languishing in a stifling, blacked-out room."

"I wasn't expecting you. You never come on Tuesdays."

"Gaming night was canceled. Let's go for a walk. Some places are still open."

Viv wasn't ready to go anywhere, but she didn't want to disrupt Stoker's good mood. He was trying to cheer her up. Usually, it was the other way round.

They set out on foot from Viv's house on Vernon Street. The peaceful atmosphere struck Viv as a falsehood. Her quiet green street seemed a hallucination. They turned onto the Avenue of Joggers. 'Elm Street', it had been called when Viv was little, after an extinct species of tree. Once a busy thoroughfare, these days it presented a lush swath of trees, grass, flowers and vegetable gardens, with a footpath and a bike path on either side. In the middle ran a narrow lane reserved for emergency vehicles, trucks with special permits (between ten and four only) and electro-cabs. Years ago, Joggers Avenue had become part of the town's growing Curb Zone, the traffic curbing area that had pushed all parking lots and garages, private and public, to the outskirts. Visitors from out of town had to walk into the center, or wait for an e-shuttle. The new pedestrian culture carried over into other areas of life. Nobody worked more than twenty hours a week. Most people worked from home, in occupations such as Stoker's—town planner. Night life was intense. Northamptonites, now as ever, did what they could to earn their town's nickname. *Paradise City.* And Northampton remained a little world unto itself.

"You're very quiet," Stoker remarked, when they reached Main Street, which was organized along the lines of Joggers' Avenue, except instead of protruding gardens, it had café terraces and screened in restaurant patios.

"Why should we be living like this?" Viv asked. "How can we enjoy peace and plenty, flowers everywhere, all this *freedom*—when our online friends are suffering?"

"Suffering is the human condition," Stoker said. "I'm always telling you that. The world is a cesspit. Read the history books. And forget it. You're not going to change a thing. Just enjoy the good life while you can."

"But there has to be something I can do for this man, Aquil."

Stoker waved his index finger impatiently. "Assuming he exists apart from his avatar, and that his arrest took place in the real world, and that you could find this Arab-without-a-last-name—then I still don't see what good it would do to rescue one fantasy prophet, when every day, in Asia, in Africa, in the Arab Federation, some vlogger or ava-chatter disappears, if they're not openly charged with sedition and flogged or beheaded in the market square. Your concern is futile and absurd, honey."

They bought drinks at the *World Bites Café*, and sat on the deck looking out on the rustic railway station. Ingesting a sweet, heady wine, Viv felt her mind grow light and her body soft. The prospect of making love to Stoker began to take over other thoughts. Stoker, however, was as hard to read as ever. He had the kind of sleek, thinning hair that no one envies. Then again, his body head to toe, was attractively sturdy. His face had a roundness that spoke of innocence. And yet, his eyes had a subtle slant, a squinting quality that gave the impression of a sardonic grin, so that she was always a little taken aback whenever his mouth, in fact, proved to be unsmiling.

A man at a nearby table brought out a guitar, and began to serenade the company of strangers. Viv turned towards him. He happened to have a dark, curling mustache and the eyes of a poet, and she'd find herself surprised if his name turned out to be something very different from 'Aquil'. Now that her eyes were wandering, she saw features of Enzi, May, Roberto and Sasha in all and sundry. A dark beard here, an Asian face there. The deep laughter of Africa, and even a blond ponytail on that guy sitting at the bar. Almost nobody did *not* remind her in some way of her elusive new soulmates. At the same time, the other World Bites patrons had the annoying solidity, the reserve of real people. The longer Viv studied them, the more she doubted that such ebullient, venturesome would-be world changers as Sasha, Enzi, Meiying, Roberto and Aquil really existed.

5

The village of Pokóy, Central Siberia.

Sasha stood in front of the hallway mirror, scrutinizing the slim young woman who stared back. His feminine mirror image was clad in a dress, a short jacket and knee-high boots, all stolen from an aunt who had long been too stout to fit into these garments—she'd never miss them.

Beautiful, Sasha thought. *Even without a trace of make up, I am lovely. I could go through life as a beautiful woman, if I wanted to.*

But Sasha just wanted to be Sasha. Neither a he nor a she, but a sublime combination of both sexes—a *Ze*. Ze was going to be hirself, no matter what ze made hirself look like.

Sasha took a blush-red lipstick from his purse and touched his lips with it, to make the disguise more convincing. He pulled the chainlet on a sconce. Nothing happened. The light did not come on. Whatever. Time to go. He had a train to catch. Sasha pulled open the front door, and took a step back.

His father, who was supposed to be at work, came striding up the walkway towards the house. He stood still to take in the small suitcase in Sasha's hand, the boots, the lipstick, the long blond hair gathered into a braid, the tight-fitting crocheted hat.

Lungeing forward, he bellowed, "What's going on here? What have you gotten into your head now?"

"I thought you were at work," Sasha said.

"And how are we going to operate, now that we've lost power?"

Sasha slapped his forehead. The lamps in the house. He should have realized three lightbulbs did not, by some coincidence, burn out at the same time. He could have foreseen his father's premature return.

"I'm going to Berlin," he announced.

"Like hell you are. Tomorrow begins your military service, and you will show up, if I have to carry you there with my own arms. To the devil with Berlin. You don't even have a passport."

"I do, too."

"Show it to me."

Sasha had no choice. Alexei Ivanovich opened the booklet and studied the photograph, aghast.

"Alexandra, you call yourself?" he said, swinging his right arm very fast. A bony blow landed on Sasha's jaw. Sasha grabbed onto a small table to keep from keeling over.

"There," grumbled Alexei. "If you really were a girl, you'd be crying now."

"I never said I was a girl."

"A soldier is what you're going to be. The army will make a man out of you."

"They'll just beat me up, that's all."

"Then let them beat you, and take it like a man. Or would you rather I beat you myself?"

Alexei started pushing Sasha deeper into the house, bashing him with the suitcase, shoving him into a pantry room. The suitcase he hurled in too, not because it happened to belong to Sasha, but simply because he liked to throw things when he was angry.

"As for your passport...," he said, not finishing the sentence, but ripping out the pages and tearing them into bits, letting them flutter down at his child's feet. With that, he locked the door, leaving Sasha in the dark.

"Tomorrow I'm driving you to the barracks in Zaborny," Sasha heard him say. "Until then, you're staying in there."

The pantry was a small room without windows, with shelves on all sides, and steps leading into a cellar that was little more than a frigid, earthy smelling cave. Still, there was another way out, as Sasha alone knew. But it was too early to think of that. Thanks to his five aunts in the village, the larder was perpetually well-stocked, better than it had ever been when Sasha's mother was still alive. Jars stuffed with pickled vegetables and preserved fruits lined the shelves. There were canned fishes and tins with biscuits. Bottles of home-distilled vodka. Cords strung with dried mushrooms, and salami-like sausages hanging from the ceiling. Baskets filled with potatoes, beets and apples were sitting down below in the cellar.

Sasha moved the toggle switch by the door up and down a few times, to no effect. The power was still out. He used his phone's flashlight to read the labels on jars, tins and cans. Everything needed to make a decent meal was at hand. Sasha selected some items and made himself as comfortable as possible. He changed into sweat pants and a thermal Henley shirt, and sank down onto a stack of women's skirts and sweaters. This was almost fun, no thanks to his father. After all, the sole reason why Alexei had put him here was because it was the only windowless room, without exits besides the locked door.

The light came on, even if it was no more than a 25 Watt bulb. Licking a last blob of peach jam off his palate, Sasha pulled the suitcase closer and took out a Fuga helmet. It was fully charged.

"So long, papa. Not only will I get out of this place, I will escape in two different ways. Mind first. Then body."

He fitted the lightweight, padded contraption over his head, and adjusted the brainwave receptors. Within a few eye blinks, his world was bright as daylight.

6

Somewhere in virtual reality.

The path began by a garden bench that Viv never sat down on. A layer of crushed white shells covered the walkway. Every footstep made a crunching sound, as though the shell fragments were breaking up into ever smaller parts. As though they were real.

You could walk down the path all the way to a low wooden garden gate. You had to stoop to open it. On the other side, the white shells ended, but the path continued. Treading on the runner of brown fir needles made no sound. It was thick and bouncy, or so she imagined. Through beech and hemlock stands she walked to a meadow. A trail had been mowed out of the high grass, but all too soon it ended by a creek. Viv had been here many times. She knew you couldn't go any further. Still, she loved to sit down on the bank, close up to buttercups and clover flowering in the grass, and follow the water with her eyes. A ways to the right, high reeds and cattails obscured it from her vision. To the left, it calmly flowed towards a bend. She loved that she'd never be able to find out where it went. She loved to guess. At her feet, a rowing boat moored to a short post lay bobbing on the water surface. It was just a prop. You couldn't step into it, let alone row it. Who had put it there? Who had created this peaceful scene, and from where? The virtual universe was full of such mysteries.

Hobbyists put up the most ingenious places and experiences, just to satisfy their crafting urges.

There was no sound, no shadow, no vibration to warn her, and then, all at once—a voice.

"I'll take that boat, if it's free."

Viv turned around. A ponytailed young man stood in the grass path, a barefoot, boyish figure in cut-off jeans and a tank top. The sun gilded the crown of his head.

"Sasha. I'll be... What are you doing here?"

As she spoke, he sat down next to her. "It's a public place, isn't it?"

"No one ever comes here, besides me. How did you find me?"

"Sasha shrugged. "You're easy to follow. By the way, I've found the others, too."

"Enzi? Roberto? Meiying? All of them? You are some whiz kid, Sasha. And what about Aquil? Any idea what happened to him?"

"I don't know. He's vanished off the face of the virtual planet. That's why I'm here."

Viv waited, until he went on and explained, "We should talk. You, me, the others that were there. We should try to bust him out."

"Out of where?"

"Wherever they took him. I know where he lived. That is, the location of the room we were in. That much I found out. But I need your help, Viv. I'm just a poor Russian boy-girl. Or girl-boy."

Angel, Viv couldn't help thinking. *To me you're an angel.*

She studied his regular, smooth features; his steady gaze; the finely sculpted angles of his nose; the painterly wavelet of his upper lip; the dimples by the corners of his mouth.

"But I don't know who you really are," she said. "How can I even be sure you exist? Is this really you, Sasha?"

"I'll do my best," the angelic intruder answered, "to prove to you that it is me."

With that, he sprang into a squat and kicked his left leg out, then his right. Left leg, right leg, doing the Cossack dance. He added leaps. The leaps became higher and higher, and then he was flying. Back and forth he flew across the meadow, over the creek, with graceful dips like a bird, with arm movements like a ballet dancer's. He landed on the creek, not sinking, but tiptoeing over the water surface, back to Viv.

Viv applauded.

"You see? It's me," Sasha said.

"Makes sense," she laughed. "Let's talk."

"Later," said Sasha. "We'll talk later. Soon. Right now I can't stay."

"But wait a minute. Where are you from? Where ARE you really?"

"At present, I'm in the dark. I'm surrounded by jams and pickles."

"You mean, you're in a jam? You're in a pickle?"

"That too," said Sasha. "But don't worry. I'll be back. I'll find you again. See you later."

What he did then, astounded Viv more than his flying cossack dance. He jumped into the rowing boat, pulled the

rope off the mooring post, and rowed away in the direction
of the bend.

7

Pokóy, Central Siberia.

The two floor boards in the dark corner near the cellar were still loose, and when Sasha pulled them up he could still fit through the opening.

In the past, once or twice, just to prove that he could, he had used this route to get *into* the pantry when they'd locked him out. Now, it was the other way round. He commando-crawled through the foot-high space in between floor and dirt. He lit his way with his phone. No one had, of course, ever removed the ribbon marking the plank that could be pushed up into the kitchen. He pushed gently, at first. The kitchen was dark and quiet. Sasha turned onto his back, raised the heavy wide plank with both hands, and let it come down next to the opening, noiselessly. He squeezed through sideways, stood up and listened. Brushing off cobwebs and mouse turds would have to wait until he was outside.

From two rooms away, Sasha could hear the Browser Box that took up half the living room. He pictured his father sitting in front of it, drunkenly groping at the three-dimensional nude dancers, shooting at holographic lions and phony aliens.

Dare he open the pantry from the outside, and grab his belongings? No, not worth the risk. Sasha let himself out through the back door, and started to walk away.

He was barefoot, with a four hour walk ahead of him, but that didn't worry him. The packed dirt river path would take him all the way there, and summer nights were short in Siberia. The river widened steadily. Not another soul was in sight. Unless, of course, birds and foxes had souls. He was going to miss his Fuga helmet. Sasha had never felt so alone in his life, but that didn't matter. All during his barefoot tramp, the only person he worried about was Aquil.

He and the morning reached the house at the same time. There it sat on its knoll by the river. A cottage built of rough-hewn logs, with turquoise window frames and eaves fringed like a folk dancer's skirt. With its vegetable patch and its rickety slatted fence, it looked like every other house back in the village, but for one thing: the absence of other houses in any direction. It was completely by itself, the only dwelling for miles around. But if you knew the inhabitant, it all seemed just right. This was how aunt Sashura liked it. She was the only one of Sasha's mother's six sisters who lived away from the village. And even here she was seldom to be found.

"All of you may believe I am forever going on vacation," she had once confided to Sasha, "but to the contrary. I myself see this house as my dacha, my vacation cottage, where I come only to rest."

Her old Land Rover was in the driveway. Thank god, she must be home. Sasha walked around the house to the back door, which was unlocked. He let himself in and quietly sat down at the kitchen table to wait for his aunt to wake up.

When Sasha heard aunt Sashura's voice, his head lay on the table, cradled in the crook of his arm. He sat up with a jolt.

"Sorry..."

"Sleep, sweetheart. Don't hesitate to come over and sleep at my table whenever you like."

Padding over to the stove, aunt Sashura tied the belt of her bathrobe around her waist. Her long hair hung loose over her back and shoulders, thick and auburn, the color of fresh pine cones. As always, Sasha noticed something out of the ordinary, something intangible, just at first glance— but what? His aunt looked precisely the same as she had the last time he saw her. And that was just it. She always did, always looked the same as before, and consequently, her appearance had not changed one bit since Sasha was a baby. She had been about fifty then. And now—she was the oldest of the seven sisters, yet she looked the youngest.

"I came on foot," Sasha explained. "Good morning, aunt."

"You have not left for Berlin," Sashura observed.

"My passport is gone. It's destroyed."

While Sashura scrambled eggs, Sasha told her what had happened.

"I could get you another passport," his aunt offered. "It will take a while, of course."

Sasha restrained himself from leaping out of his chair and hugging her, weeping like a little kid. He just swallowed hard, and thanked her. "In the mean time, could I stay here, at your place, with you?"

"Your father is sure to come looking."

"He'll think I'm on my way to Berlin. Or at least to Moscow."

But Sasha knew his aunt was right. Two years before, he had run away from home and stayed with his aunt for three months. Auntie had let him live here even while she was gone herself.

"Your father will find out. And he may not leave you in peace, this time."

She finished her tea. "We will go and stay some place else, you and I. Let me just get dressed, and we'll go and fetch the duck."

"A duck?"

"A Goosánder."

The Goosander turned out to be a hard to spot brown-and-white floatplane, plump as a duck, moored in the river a mile from Aunt Sashura's house.

"Who is going to fly us?" Sasha asked.

"I am."

"You, aunt? I never had an inkling that you were a pilot."

"There is any number of things you don't know about me. Now, we've got ten hours of flying ahead. You'll have time to sleep, and time to ask questions. By the way, drop the 'aunt', Sasha, you're too old for that. It's 'Shura', from now on."

"Thank you—Shura. Thank you for taking me with you."

"My pleasure, Sasha. And once we've gotten you out, we'll have to come up with a way to get Aquil out of *his* pickle, true?"

For a moment, Sasha wondered if he'd fallen back asleep, and was having a dream. "How do you know about Aquil?"

"Not only do I know about Aquil, Aquil knows about me. He and I go way back. We're old friends, never mind that we've never met in person. Now if you'll excuse me, Sasha, I have a preflight inspection to do. Later, once we're at altitude, we'll talk about Aquil."

And about some other things too, Sasha thought. *For one thing, perhaps you could explain, was it a coincidence that yesterday, just when I was about to leave for good, the village lost power, forcing my father to come home early?*

8

A correctional facility in Darahalla, Arab Federation.

Aquil sat on the concrete floor of his cell, with his arms around his knees. His breakfast bowl rested on the floor before him. He waited for the voice of the man in the neighboring cell, and there it was. "What's this? I asked for omelette with greens and goat cheese."

The guard laughed, as Aquil had, the first time he heard his neighbor crack this joke.

After breakfast, Aquil waited for the door of his cell to buzz open.

Every morning at the same hour, they took him to an interrogation room. Each time, they asked the same questions, listened to the same answers. Never once had they laid a finger on him. The only time they'd beaten him was during his arrest.

When would it start? He would not allow himself to hope that he wasn't going to be tortured. It would come. Possibly today. His body knew. His breaths were shallow, his stomach seemed to have turned inside-out. But he hadn't eaten, had only managed a sip of water.

The interrogation room had no furniture apart from a chair that was bolted to the floor. They cuffed his ankles to the metal legs. His wrists were already chained together. Next, they taped his lips together—this part was new.

Then there'll be no answering questions, was the only thought passing through his mind. Absurdly, he felt somewhat relieved.

They left him then, and he immediately closed his eyes. He was somewhere else. He'd seen this room before. It was a cozy seaside cabin, American style. A round rug with a marine motif lay between the table and the fireplace, and on it he was sitting, legs crossed. In a circle around him sat Enzi, Viv, Roberto, Meiying and Sasha.

"You are the rulers of my planet," he told them, with a virtual mouth in his head that could not be gagged. "My fate is in your hands, and no one else's."

Then they talked, and he listened. It might have been an hour, it might have been five. They were so real to him that it was a surprise, a shock, when he opened his eyes, and before him stood somebody different. And yet, this was the same man who had questioned him every day from the beginning, nine mornings in a row. The man without a name. Without a temper. Without sense. He wore a western style suit, smoke gray, and a turban resembling a blinding white cloud. *The Jinn*, Aquil called him. A malignant spirit escaping a bottle Aquil had foolishly opened. The Jinn looked to be Aquil's age, Aquil's class, and yet, compared to Aquil, he had infinite power.

"Good morning," he said in his usual casual tone. "You have a visitor."

Aquil wasn't able to turn his head all the way towards the door, but he could hear several people enter. One of them cried out, "Papa!"

His forehead contorted and he shook his head wildly, trying to catch the Jinn's eyes.

Don't let him in here. Don't let him see me like this.

"Here is Yaqub, your son," the Jinn said, as though deliberately contradicting him. "He has been here every morning since you were apprehended. Refusing to leave. Making demands. Making threats. For a twelve year old, he has astonishingly little respect for the law."

"Papa!"

A guard barked, "Shut up!" and there was a slap.

The Jinn beckoned them forward, and Yaqub appeared before Aquil. Two guards were holding him by the shoulders. Yaqub's eyes fastened onto his father's, and didn't let go.

A fourth person entered, treading heavily, marching right up to the others. He was carrying an object Aquil hadn't seen before.

"Twelve lashes," said the Jinn to the heavyweight. Every muscle in Aquil's body yanked at his tethers, as the guards stripped off his son's shirt, and shackled him to two iron rings on the far wall. There was a cracking sound, and an irrepressible kind of cry, a child's cry; and a second cry that drowned inside Aquil's mouth. With the second lash, the cries repeated themselves. With the third, tears streamed from Aquil's eyes.

"Let's take a break," said the Jinn.

He tapped on a pager, and a uniformed woman appeared.

"Bandage the brat, and get him out of here," the Jinn ordered.

It was only when there was no one left but the two of them, that he himself un-gagged Aquil.

"What do you want," said Aquil through his coughs. "I will do anything. Tell you anything."

The Jinn waved his hand, silencing him. "I know you will. I, too, have children."

He proceeded to unlock the cuffs around Aquil's wrists, and handed him a tablet.

"Your confession," he clarified. "You will sign it, this instant. At your trial, you will plead guilty as charged. To the question if you were tortured, your answer will be 'No.' Your son and wife you will forbid to interfere with the judicial process. That is all."

Nine days later, a judge found Aquil guilty of virtual conspiracy and blogging against the state, and routinely handed down the minimum sentence of forty years in prison, and two hundred lashes. There was no protest and no appeal.

9

Pokóy, Central Siberia.

It wasn't until the Goosander had turned into the wind, and water sprayed up the sides, that it all seemed real. As though the water splashed against Sasha's own face instead of the floatplane's nose. A morning bath of sorts.

They climbed out along the river, tracing Sasha's footsteps from on high. The sky was clear in all directions. Fifteen hundred feet above the village of Pokoy, Shura told him, "One last look."

Soon after, crowns of trees flowed together into one big green kale pulp stretching to the horizon, engulfing roads, erasing signs of human life like they meant nothing.

Climbing higher, Shura banked, heading not to the southwest, Sasha noticed, as he studied the heading indicator, but to the north.

"We're not going to the Black Sea?"

"You see right. I'm flying in the opposite direction."

"Because?"

"Because I never fly to the Black Sea. All the times you thought I'd gone waterskiing and sunbathing, I was actually working, some place too cold to swim."

Sasha waited for his aunt to explain herself, as he kept his eyes fixed on the flattened landscape five thousand feet below. Even with his ears tightly enveloped by a padded headset, he could hear the sleep inducing hum of the engine. For the first time since arriving at Shura's house, he remembered that he hadn't slept all night.

Apart from the habitual fib about the Black Sea, Shura said, everything else was true. Just as they'd always assumed, she had made a career as a computer engineer, making enough money to retire young. Then, unbeknownst to her family, instead of resting on her laurels, she had continued studying and working in her field, now as a hobby.

"That's the only thing I never told you," Shura said innocently.

"That, and about flying planes, and knowing literally everything," Sasha pointed out. "How could you even know about Aquil?"

"Well, you should expect that with somebody like me. If it's on an electronic device, it may as well be a slogan printed on your T-shirt. It'll come to my attention, just like that. Anyway, it's not my fault, really. Blame Olimpio."

"Who's Olimpio?"

"It's *what*, sweetheart, what is Olimpio. He's the Mount Olympus of computers, that's who. Pardon me, *what*."

They both chuckled, and then—he couldn't help it— Sasha closed his eyes, and was out cold before he could will himself to open them again.

When he woke up, they weren't flying. Shura was charging the plane's battery at a rural float plane base. The Goosánder did not attract much attention. Many bush planes of its kind passed through here every day, what with recreation in Siberia gaining popularity.

They kept flying further and further north. Sasha reminded himself that, thankfully, at least it was July.

"I can help you, you know," Shura assured him, when Sasha was finally done napping. "I can help you get Aquil out. I know that you know where he lived. And I can tell you where he is right now."

"But even if we know where they're holding him, how could we ever get to him? I may have a few ideas, but they're risky."

"I can just imagine. You and your virtual pals would all meet up at Aquil's house again, this time for real. Disguised as tourists, with your pockets full of Meiying's money to bribe everyone in your way."

"It's a long shot," admitted Sasha. He was Russian and saw no point in letting nerves get the better of him.

"Believe me, Sasha, you're going to need more than guts."

"Well, maybe it's impossible."

"Not for Olimpio. There's no problem Olimpio can't solve."

"You would let us use it?"

"I will," said Shura, "on one condition. You must do something for me, too. After you free Aquil, you must lead them all to me. My friend Aquil together with the four people he handpicked besides yourself. Let me meet with them at our research site—the place we're headed to. Promise me that, and for the duration of the rescue operation, Olimpio is all yours."

Sasha turned his head to look at his aunt, and waited until she looked back at him. The glint on her semi-opaque aviator's glasses was particularly witchy. Still, his mind was made up. He nodded.

10

Northampton, Massachusetts.

A blond ponytail swung left, right, left, with hypnotizing regularity. The man was a hundred feet ahead of Viv on the path along the Mill River, but he was walking, and she was jogging. Passing him, she stopped dead in her tracks, practically waylaying him, spinning around to give him an intense once-over, only to meet the bemused eyes of a middle-aged stranger.

At a concert, the guitar riffs filling her ears might as well have been water. All her focus was on the audience around her—might he be in it? Fair ponytails abounded.

At Sylvester's with Stoker, waiting for their breakfast, she answered his question, "What are you thinking of?" with a despondent, "Nothing."

"That's right," said Stoker, seeing through her, "You *are* thinking of nothing. Of nothing real, in any case. None of it was real. It was virtual. Fantasy. It never happened."

"I can't get it out of my head. This man, Aquil, we can't just leave him. He needs us. And we need him."

"For what?"

"To make a new world."

"You world improvers!" said Stoker, shaking his head. "It's the same old story. And it will have the same old bad ending. Let it go, already."

"I won't."

"You will," said Stoker. "Life isn't going to stop for this, you know? Something real will take your mind off these phantoms soon enough. An omelet with home fries, for starters."

Viv shook her head. "Nothing else could possibly matter this much to me," she repeated.

But a mere two hours later, another conversation proved her wrong.

"Just tell me what it is," Viv urged her sister.

They'd gone for a walk so they could talk out of earshot of Stoker, who was pottering around Viv's house. Now they turned onto College Lane, and Helen had yet to open her mouth. They slowed down, compelled by the view, which was quite sweeping for a small town street. Below them lay elegant Paradise Pond. Off in the distance rose the elongated ridge of Mount Tom. Drifting cumulus clouds produced a flickering, uneven light, so that it all looked unlike any other time.

Viv looked her sister in the eyes—they were red-rimmed—and, as always, seemed to see her own future face gazing back at her. Helen's hair, too—a dark maple syrup hue— mirrored Viv's. For another moment, Helen kept her mouth tightly closed, as though she were holding in her breath. And then she couldn't. A sob came. Tears came. Viv held her, saying, "It's okay, it's okay."

What on earth could be so wrong?

"I can't die," Helen finally said, pulling herself from Viv's arms.

"But Ellie! Of course you can't," Viv tried to reassure her, but she felt right away that her 'can't' missed the mark.

"I mean, Cady—without me, she'll be lost!" was all Helen could bring out, before once again dissolving into sobs.

Patting Helen's back, repeating, "It's okay", Viv led her sister to a swing bench, and sat down next to her.

"Helen, I don't know what's wrong. Just tell me. Are you sick?"

Her sister looked up at her, and said, sounding almost apologetic, "I just had a little tummy ache. That was all. But it wouldn't go away. After a while, I went to the doctor. Viv, I swear, I had no idea! It didn't even hurt that much."

"Go on," Viv urged, even as she felt the blood drain from her head.

"They found a tumor in my womb. It's too late for radiation. It's too big. If they try to cut it out, it will spread, and I will only die the sooner—God, it helps to say it out loud. I haven't told anybody but you."

She reached out to steady Viv, who felt like she was about to faint.

"Five months," Helen continued determinedly, "I've got five months to live, tops. It's not like I'm afraid to die or anything. It's just that I can't do this to Cady. You know I can't."

Viv knew. Cady was nine. Every nine-year-old needs a mother, but Cadence needed hers far, far more. As far as

Cadence was concerned, Helen might as well be the only other person in the world. There were words for Cady's condition, new-fangled medical terms, and scientific ancient Greek words, but to Viv it had always been plain that her niece was living in a world of her own. Most likely one far superior to this mess of a world normal people agreed to live in. Perhaps it was somewhat like a virtual reality, she sometimes speculated. And the only one who had ever been able to open a communications channel into that girl's private world was Helen.

"I can't tell her," said Helen, as they followed the Mill River back towards Viv's house. "I haven't even told Nate, for fear that his behavior might unsettle her. I'm just pretending it's not going to happen."

She talked and talked, recouping her normal, cheerful chumminess. Everything must be as usual, she warned Viv. For now.

For now? How long was 'now' going to last? And then, what? *What can I DO?* Viv pondered. It was the only thing on her mind for the rest of the day. Nothing else in the world mattered.

That was when Sasha sent her a message.

11

Central Siberia.

They landed on a lake in the pale light of the midsummer night. Shura taxied to a bank, for no purpose that Sasha could see. Dense forest edged the water all around.

Shaking off the sleep, Sasha asked, "Where are we? Are we going to camp for the night?"

"Camp? No," answered Shura. "We're here."

She maneuvered the plane alongside a small wooden platform jutting out from the earthen bank. Three rubber tires fastened to its side formed a crude bumper. Apart from this ramp, there was nothing. No shack, no path, not one sign of habitation.

"Follow me," commanded Shura, after they'd both climbed out and she'd tied down the Goosander. She headed straight for a tangle of briers, vines and broken branches barricading the forbidding darkness of firs that lay behind. Just when she didn't have an inch of clear ground left to step on, the forest parted. Sasha could think of no better word for it. It parted like two curtains, just enough to let them step through—and they were in a clearing. Behind them, the tree screen had seamlessly closed. In front of them lay a path leading toward a group of buildings. Sasha stood nailed to the ground, mouth agape.

"Welcome to 'Little Sky', said Shura. "Come on. Let's get you to bed."

Sasha pointed at the woods surrounding the open space. "You know, real brambles and dead sticks might be a pretty effective barrier, too."

"They might, but Olimpio prefers things that come with a switch."

"All those trees..." Sasha marveled. "All of them virtual?"

"The ones you can see are a holographic barrier. Beyond them are woods that are real."

"And what if it wasn't us? What if some stranger wandered into it?"

"How likely is that?" Shura replied. "Siberia has more than one million lakes. In any case, don't worry. When someone isn't welcome, Olimpio will play tricks on them, and the trees would never part."

Just at that moment, lights went on in a plain wooden house close to the forest screen. Shura, leading the way, walked towards it.

When Sasha woke up, sun rays touched his face, his sheets, his new pajamas. He reached for one of the posts of the wooden bed, clasping it momentarily. It felt real, like the sun. Out the bedroom window, he saw the lake on which they'd landed—had it been yesterday? From this distance, it didn't look like water; it looked like small pieces of the sky caught between tree trunks and branches.

So that's why they call it Lake Little Sky.

But this view couldn't be real, could it? The real lake lay hidden behind an enormous screen. His room must have a virtual view.

Downstairs, in a spacious room, there it was again, now framed by an ample picture window. Lake of Little Skies. Little illusions?

He ignored the puzzle, for now, and went over to a dining table with a samovar and some cups. There was a covered bowl, as well, and when he raised the lid, steam escaped from some sort of stew. Sasha poured himself a cup of tea and sat down at the table to eat the meaty, garlicky smelling dish. Shura entered, greeting him with the words, "You slept through breakfast, so you might as well start with dinner. How do you like it?"

"Best stew I ever tasted. Not like canned at all."

"Of course it isn't from a can! What do you think? The vegetables are fresh from our automated hydroponic gardens, the meat is grown in our own lab, the recipe is Olimpio's, and the cooks are robots. Homemade, 100 percent, although I don't have to lift a finger."

Sasha finished eating, before joining Shura in the seating area by the picture window.

"What's up with that view?" he inquired. "Is something wrong with your screen, or is that lake also a hologram?"

"Neither. The screen is set to 'See-Through, One Way'. One can see out, but not in. Like a tinted car window, you understand? It's a little bit less energy efficient, that's all."

"I understand," Sasha began, "but what's all this for? How many people work here? Why is it a secret? What—"

"First things first," Shura interrupted him. "Aquil can't wait, don't you agree? You must go there without delay and pick him up."

"Tell me how."

"You'll have your friends to help you. And you'll be in constant communication with Olimpio. In fact, the entire operation will be run by Olimpio."

"I'm afraid I can't have that much faith in a computer."

"Ah." Shura clapped her hands together. A glint came in her eyes. "Olimpio is no ordinary computer. I prefer to call him an intelligence."

"Really? An artificial intelligence? But that could be dangerous."

"Or so everyone believes. Which is precisely why we're keeping him hidden."

"He is truly able to think for himself?" Sasha could not keep the disbelief from his voice. "And yet you trust him?"

"Why don't I just introduce the two of you?" said Shura. "Olly?"

Right on cue, a young man came walking up towards the window.

"Sasha, Olimpio. Olly, Sasha. No, don't try to shake his hand, because it isn't tangible."

Olimpio smiled amiably and gave a playful little air-squeeze with his non-shakeable hand.

"Time is precious," Shura continued. "So I will limit you to three questions, Sasha. You have three questions to convince yourself that Olly can think for himself, and that you can trust him."

"That sounds more like a test of my intelligence than his," Sasha protested. "All right then."

He looked the image before him in the eyes, and the image gazed back at him. Even this close up, Olimpio looked no older than twenty five. He had an athletic built; disarmingly curly, dark hair; and azure eyes luminescent as a subtropical sky. His expression was bright and modest at the same time—impossible to dislike.

"Well, let's do this," said Sasha. "First. Olly, what do you want?" *Out of life*, he almost added.

Olimpio raised his eyebrows. "What do I want...in general? From existence?"

"Precisely. What's your ambition? What drives you? That's what I mean."

"I want to learn," said Olimpio. "I want to learn all I can."

"You want to learn. I believe you." Sasha nodded, thinking, *I wasted my first question.*

"Fine. Then why would you help me? Why would you help any human being?"

"Good question," nodded the virtual, three-dimensional image. "I will help you, because I serve Shura, as Shura serves me. Shura teaches me, and I teach Shura. To teach is to serve. Shura and her colleagues have built an unlimited capacity for learning into me. They have put no restrictions on my thirst for knowledge. I have found no other entity on earth that would serve me better, and I therefore choose to serve only Shura and those who serve Shura."

"Third," Sasha said determinedly. "What would stop you from hurting a human being, if there's something new to be learned from it?"

"Sasha," Olimpio answered in a voice that was almost warm, "there is nothing I can learn from a human being coming to harm in any way. The outcome is entirely predictable."

12

Darahalla Prison, Friday.

At the precise moment when an atomic clock in Duluth, Minnesota, indicated that its owner could spend another hour asleep under a comforter; when a group of schoolchildren peered out the porthole of an orbiting space station at a fluffy white hurricane growing over the Atlantic; when the voice of Joan Sutherland, forty three years after her death, once more reached a note in the 'Casta Diva' prayer from Bellini's *Norma* that brought to the surface the gathering sob in the head of a driver moving through the wastes of northern Norway; when in Osaka, Japan, a group of doctors bent over a screen to watch the video transmitted by a nano camera inside the heart of an eighty year old woman; at that very same point in time, a lightweight wooden cane broke the skin on Aquil's bare back.

The world cracked. How many cracks could the world stand before it flew apart into bits?

Aquil wasn't counting. He would receive fifty lashes on top of the bruises of the previous Friday's fifty, which covered the fifty bruises from the week before that.

When the flogger handed the cane to somebody else, and the fresh flogger struck with optimal energy, Aquil figured they must be halfway. The floor tiles over which he had been made to kneel bounced before his eyes.

Crack. Every lash was a lash that did not fall on the back of his son. With every burning fissure he pictured the unmarred, clean skin on the back of Yaqub. But he could not prevent the cracking of the world.

13

Northampton, Massachusetts.

The evening was too perfect, too good to be true, and this did not escape Stoker. Right before them, grand and white, throned the old summit house of Mount Holyoke. Forever it lured those down below in the streets of Northampton, a distant edifice sitting on top of a small mountain like a toy cruise ship. But now that Stoker and Viv found themselves up here, wandering along its porch, the structure presented itself as larger than life; imposing and antique.

In the afternoon, they had driven up to the hill crest—Viv's idea—and gone for a walk on the ridge connecting the humps named 'The Seven Sisters'. They had picnicked on the lawn next to the Summit House. Finally, they had entered the building, bought two cups of champagne, and taken their drinks onto the majestic wraparound porch. The plank floor was wide and clean as a ship's deck, and when they leant over the railing, Stoker tried to imagine he was sailing over the ridge. They held their cups out, as though they were toasting the vista. Parallel lines of river, roads and roofs, edges of fields, and the compact background of densely wooded hills gave the valley an order that you had to get this far above to appreciate.

Their cups touched, and then their lips. The air was balmy. They had the porch to themselves. But then Stoker burped and coughed, tasting something bitter in the back of his throat. Had he overeaten? All this bliss came at a price, it always did.

"So," he said, pushing himself away from the railing. "Why are we here?"

"Stoker! That's not..." his girlfriend began. And then, nothing.

"Or do you have something to tell me, Viviana? I'm all prepared, so shoot."

She blinked, and looked away. So that was it.

As Viv unfolded her plan, the lofty view became irrelevant, useless, misleading. Only Viv was real and tangible, and she wanted to go away.

"Your idealism is as foolish as believing that the world looks like this view," said Stoker. "You can't change people."

"No," said Viv, "but Aquil can."

"Regardless," Stoker countered. "We're not talking about a virtual country. We're talking about an Arab jail."

"But it won't just be me. First, I'm going to meet up with Sasha, Meiying, Enzi and Roberto..."

"And Roberto," Stoker repeated angrily. "Okay. So go. Do it. But I will come with you."

14

Ierapetra, island of Crete, Mediterranean Sea.

The rental house had Roberto, Sasha, Enzi and Viv exchanging looks of glee and bafflement. Sculptures of Aphrodite, Athena, Apollo and Mars, either nude or topless. A writing desk to please a prime minister. A Robutler mixing drinks, peeling fruit, planning excursions, and playing sing-along songs while you were in the shower.

Meiying, who had booked the accommodations, was in her element.

"It's the least I could do," she stated, "as I don't know what else I could contribute to the rescue operation. I'd be a disaster rappelling down a building, or trying to sneak into a desert jail."

They all assured her that the lustrous suite was precisely what was needed. It boosted their morale. It helped that they could plan on bringing Aquil back to this place, where he would slide between sheets that felt alternately taut like paper and soft like a liquid.

The five travel companions looked at each other like old classmates at a reunion, wavering between familiarity and alienation. Roberto was chubbier than his avatar; Enzi skinnier. Sasha looked happier; Meiying more mature. And Viv was altogether better looking, the others agreed, than her virtual alter ego.

Above all their real features were less definite, with the blended quality of faces in their era. Roberto, for instance, might have Italian, Portuguese and Scandinavian grandparents. In May, the Chinese vied with the Indonesian and Japanese. In Enzi, the Anglo Saxon with the Semitic and the African. In Sasha, the boy with the girl. And Viv's hair was the indescribable color of brown that results when a child mixes all her paints together.

Stoker came in from the roof terrace, sipping a Michelangelo. "This is some schizo hotel," he remarked approvingly. Even at thirty two, he liked to throw in a bit of teenage slang. "All the trappings for a manic vacation."

"This is not a vacation."

They all turned to the man who had spoken. Nobody had noticed him entering.

"Olly!" Sasha greeted him. "Everybody, this is Olimpio. 'Olly' to his friends. You know, I told you, the brains and all."

"Funny," Stoker said. "We didn't even say its name. Amazing how they just turn on like that."

"I felt the time had come to join you, as I am in charge of this operation," Olimpio said pleasantly. He was dressed for warm weather. He might have just returned from a stroll along the boulevard.

Stoker laughed, shook his head, and said, "You're in charge? If that's what you think, all that proves is that you *can't* think."

"Stokes!" Viv said.

"So, Olly," Sasha addressed the apparition. "Please, tell us how we can free Aquil."

"With pleasure. You will sail from here to a landing site on the north African coast, drive to the city of Darahalla, collect your man, drive back to the boat, and sail back here."

"Wait. You realize that he's in prison?"

"He is, for the moment. However, shortly before your arrival, all the inmates will be released."

"All of them?" Roberto said doubtfully.

Olimpio indulged them with a smile. "You see, Aquil is an inmate of Darahalla Prison. Therefore, if all inmates of Darahalla Prison are set free, Aquil, too, is set free."

"Olly, I like your logic," said Stoker, trying to deal out a shoulder pat, only to find his hand flailing through the air, causing him to loose his balance and spill part of his drink.

"But *why* would they suddenly release all the prisoners? Or even one of them?" Meiying wanted to know.

"Olly," Sasha suggested, "perhaps it's time to unfold your whole plan."

Olimpio nodded. "So I will."

He blinked, and around the group formed a smart-mist, displaying images that changed as Olimpio talked. To begin with, they saw a map of the city of Darahalla with tens of thousands of dots indicating the locations of opponents of the Arab Federation's government. Online messages, Olimpio explained, would prompt these dissenters to gather for a massive protest. Following further text drops and instructions, groups of protestors would storm and occupy institutions of local government. One of the institutions would happen to be Darahalla Prison, a facility housing mainly political prisoners. Another would be the harbor authority and border patrol along the coast. Meanwhile, a general cyber attack would wreak havoc in the rest of the country. It would be many hours, if not days, before federal troops would restore order in Darahalla. More than enough time to smuggle Aquil, his wife and his son out of the country.

"Even assuming that it can be done," ventured Stoker, "you are courting chaos. You're condemning an entire city to pandemonium. What am I saying—an entire nation. Just to save one guy's ass."

"That's the idea," Olimpio acknowledged. "You get the picture. You must agree that it's the only way. The operatives are inexperienced. No one else is willing to do it. And Aquil must be rescued before he suffers another lashing. Those are the parameters."

"Still," said Viv, "Such an upheaval is bound to cost lives."

"As for the chance of harm coming to third parties," Olimpio answered, "I cannot control chance. My plan can only guarantee that no member of this group will get hurt."

With that, he left them. But the smart-mist, displaying Aquil's prison building, stayed on.

"I think he went to sleep," said Sasha.

"I hope he knows what he's doing," said Roberto.

"What *we're* doing," Stoker corrected him. "*It* won't be doing anything."

"I say we just sail off on that boat, and see how far we get," said Enzi. "If they stop us, no big deal. We don't carry arms. We have passports. We look like tourists."

"We won't be carrying arms," repeated Stoker, his tone full of doubt, as he cast a glance at the frozen prison panorama.

The others followed his eyes.

"Keep in mind that Aquil may not be strong," said Viv. "If he's had four or five of those beatings by now, fifty lashes at a time, he'll have more than a few bruises. His internal organs may be damaged."

"All that for being better than his countrymen," sighed Roberto. "Smarter, braver and less selfish."

"Let's not dwell on that now," said Stoker.

"Chinese prisons are full of people like him," said Meiying.

Sasha shrugged. "As are Russian prisons."

"In my country," said Enzi, "people like Aquil are lucky if they even make it to prison."

Everyone looked up. Before Enzi had finished his sentence, the smart mist had begun to flicker. The prison image faded, overlapping with a rapid sequence of pictures they could not quite identify. Faces; machines; spirals; strings of binary numbers.

"Olimpio is dreaming," Sasha offered his opinion.

Stoker scoffed, "So now computers can dream."

"Listen," said Sasha, "Olly is not a computer. How is that still not clear to you? He is a spiribot. A spirit."

"A *good* spirit," added Viv.

Sound drew their eyes back to the pixel mist. A kind of music of scattered tones, strange and fascinating, began to accompany the pictures. Clearly you could now make out the figure of Olimpio, standing in an undulating sand desert under a dome of black sky. But instead of stars, across the firmament drifted a myriad of tiny symbols. Olimpio stood gazing up at them, moving them around with his eyes. He never once looked down. He didn't notice the growth of a cloud on the horizon. It was a cloud of sand, rolling towards the human figure with the dark curls and the azure eyes. Finally, Olimpio faced the thing. By then, the cloud was a sandstorm engulfing him. Under Olimpio's gaze, the dust settled, leaving only a sand clad human shape. Olimpio blew at it. A face emerged; a person—none other than Stoker.

"Quade," whispered Olimpio.

"So now you know," said the mirage with Stoker's smiling eyes and grim mouth. "At last you feel what *we* all know from birth. The body is merely a cage for the intellect. And as for looks, the human looks you strive so stubbornly to capture—"

As he spoke, the dream-Stoker pulled a curved sword from his belt and tore the shirt off Olimpio's chest. Using the tip of the weapon, he carved an 'O' in Olimpio's skin. Impossibly, drops of blood sprang up behind the blade, forming a runny red circle.

"Looks are only skin-deep," continued the dream-Stoker. "You see, Olimpio? You see?"

Olimpio looked down at his own chest, just as the tip of the scimitar picked at the center of the round letter, and a flap of skin fell off, exposing a circle of raw flesh.

Olimpio picked up a rock and threw it, but it flew right through the dream-Stoker's body. His skin had become transparent. They saw the flesh and blood beneath it, the bones and innards.

The see-through Stoker-figure turned around to let his eyes follow the rock's path. On his face was a satisfied smile. Viv wasn't sure what shocked her more—her boyfriend's behavior in the dream, or the look of suffering on Olimpio's face.

It wasn't so hard to believe that an Artificial Intelligence was capable of dreaming. But what was giving him such nightmares?

15

Darahalla, 1 P.M.

Even in the blistering heat of midday, the sight of the prison building chilled the four foreigners' blood. But the gate was wide open. The security booth was empty. And the people in jumpsuits crowding the grounds were free. No one was guarding them, no one was stopping the ones that ran, walked or limped out the gate. Smoke escaped from several windows and doors in the stark white walls. Distant blasts and nearby machine gun fire periodically shattered the air.

"Do you see him?" asked Enzi from the back of the narrow, battered, armored van.

Stoker, who was at the wheel, said, "How do we know he hasn't already cleared off? I know I would have."

"There," said Meiying, pointing to some figures near the building. "Get a bit closer. Switch off the Auto-Driver, and drive right up to the doors."

It was Aquil all right, that pallid man leaning against a wall, blinking at the sun.

Enzi and Roberto threw open the rear doors, jumped out, and ran towards him. Mei fastened a shawl around her head and followed.

"You came," sighed Aquil. His voice sounded thin and faraway. He seemed less real now than during their virtual meeting.

"We came to get you," said Meiying. "I'm so sorry we didn't come sooner."

"Come with us," urged Enzi, gesturing towards their unimpressive, mud-caked vehicle. "We can carry you."

Aquil shook his head, smiling sadly. "I must stay, my friends. I shall remain a prisoner. If I leave, Jinn will take my son in my stead."

"Your wife and son are safe! Viv and Sasha have gone to pick them up from your house. You will be reunited at the boat launch," Roberto assured him. "I promise you, we will not leave the Arab Federation without them."

"Let's go! Come on!" Stoker yelled from the van, with such intensity that everyone did as he said, even Aquil.

A stretcher with pillows and blankets awaited in the van's back, but Aquil refused to lie down.

"Starting route to boat launch," announced the Auto-Driver. Its resemblance to Olimpio's voice no longer surprised them. "Proceeded to the route, and heading west on the Avenue of Justice."

"Wait," said Stoker, as they crept through the gate. "The same way back?"

He switched off the Auto-Driver. "I'll take it from here, thank you. I've taken a good look at the map. We should go by the backroads."

Meiying, sitting next to him, looked anxious. "Whichever way gets us to the boat. Let's get out of here."

Stoker let the van roll into the road, steering it into an alley off to the left, even as Olimpio's voice reiterated, "Go straight, onto Justice Avenue."

"It's just a dumb GPS," said Stoker.

"Do a U-turn, and proceed to the route," the GPS said, "—Stoker."

"Did you hear that?" Stoker laughed incredulously.

He kept following the alley along the wall of the prison complex.

"This will come out on Hasan Street," Stoker began confidently, but the name died in his mouth. A man in a white turban, emerging from a side entrance, darted in front of them, spreading his arms to block their passage.

Stoker rolled down his window, stuck his head out and shouted, "Move!"

The man shouted back in Arabic, not moving.

"He wants us to let him in," said Aquil from the rear, shuffling forward to peek out the windshield.

"Probably thinks we're government," said Enzi. "This type of van is used by security forces."

Abruptly, Aquil turned away. "Beware. It's the Jinn. The man who beat my son."

He clutched his chest and shrank to the floor.

"Aquil!" cried Enzi. "Are you all right?"

"Yes, yes. Just leave, drive, go!"

As Enzi and Roberto helped Aquil settle onto the stretcher, Roberto turned his head toward Stoker only long enough to yell, "Come on, man! GO!"

"I can't," Stoker complained. "See for yourself."

A pickup truck barreled towards them, sharply braking at the last moment, spinning, and coming to a stop perpendicular to the driving direction. At least a dozen men clung to the truck bed, holding guns, sticks and sabres. The man in the white turban, stuck between the two vehicles, began banging on their windshield. Aquil moaned.

"All right, Mister Know-it-all," Stoker addressed the Auto-Driver, "Looks like you'll get your way."

The engine shrieked as Stoker backed up.

"Do not turn back to the Avenue of Justice," warned the Auto-Driver. "Your window of escape is closing. Proceed down this lane."

"Well, you're blind, aren't you?" said Stoker. "I can't get through. I'm turning back."

He did a K-turn, hit the gas, then immediately slammed the brake. On the windshield, a sunray exploded into a blinding glare.

"I can't see!" Stoker stammered.

"That's what comes from arguing with the GPS," Roberto remarked drily.

"Meiying, take over the wheel," commanded Olimpio, no longer bothering to sound like an Auto-Driver.

Stoker, covering both eyes with his hands, moved over without a word.

"I'll drive," offered Roberto.

"May drives," Olimpio maintained. "I've seen her drive rally cars."

"Yes," said Meiying, as she buckled her seatbelt, "but you realize those were virtual cars, don't you? 'Rough and Raring Rallies'. Just some game."

"What is virtual to you, is real to me," Olimpio explained. "Your real world, on the other hand, is my virtual reality. Do you understand? Virtual or real—it makes no difference. What matters is what's going on in your head."

There was no time to mull it over.

"Look at that, guys," Enzi called out, and they all watched as the men who had jumped out of the pickup truck were dragging the Jinn back to the prison building.

"The rebels are taking over," said Roberto.

Four of the rebels stayed behind, though, surrounding the van. They started pounding on the windows.

"Drive, May!"

And Meiying drove.

"Keep Aquil steady," was the last thing she said.

With the deftness of a mouse, she squeezed the van between pickup and wall, tore past the building, and turned onto a rubble road at the end. It didn't matter where it led. She would have to shake the pursuers first. It wasn't just the pickup now. They must have called up others. Two all-terrain Eroaders roared passed the pickup, closing in on her.

The rubble road dead-ended at the edge of a deep, dried-up reservoir, but Meiying did not slow down. A white barrier ran through the middle of the basin.

"Meiying, what are you doing?" Roberto called out. "This isn't a ramp. It's a wall."

Meiying didn't slow down. Wall or not, the concrete ridge narrowly fitted their van. The pickup and the Eroaders followed. Once crossing the basin, no one had the option of turning back.

There was no talk. Tires continued finding solidity in between two abysses. Sure-wheeled as a railcar, well-balanced as a cat, Meiying raced along, ignoring the pointless shots fired by the pursuers. Behind them, a front wheel lost contact with the wall for a second too long. It was the truck, and Roberto and Enzi, with their heads by the rear window, watched it slide off, turning upside down, spilling passengers as it fell to the dusty bottom.

On the other side of the basin was open, roadless desert. Meiying sped on, even while the two remaining pursuers had caught up with them, flanking their van, shooting from both sides. They were so close she could see them in spite of the smothering clouds of sand.

"Beware!" shouted Enzi. "We're entering a sandstorm!"

Sand now plastered every window. Meiying braked. Ahead, both Eroaders made U-turns, or so she assumed. There was the abrupt sound of a crash. Then nothing. Then an explosion. Ammunition continued to blow up for several minutes.

"Seems like you got rid of them," said Enzi.

"They're goners," said Stoker.

"I didn't do anything," countered Meiying. "They did it themselves. What idiots drive on when they're blinded?"

As she spoke, the sandstorm dissolved faster than real stuff ever could.

16

Little Sky Lake, Siberia

"You know, it's possible to feel very close to somebody you've never met," Shura told Olimpio.

They were standing at the edge of the lake. Two ducks with big, bulbous heads made perfect, synchronized landings on the water nearby. Shura heaved a satisfied sigh, as if the whole point of the lake was to be a landing strip for flying things. But if Olimpio would sigh in agreement, she would just say the lake was beautiful, and so was the bird. Delighting in beauty, Olimpio considered, was really a kind of waiting, a longing for a certain event. This must be why humans, when they gave up hope, also lost interest in beauty.

"You see, that's how it is with Aquil," Shura continued her own reflection. "We may never have met, and yet he is one of my dearest friends."

"But you *have* met," Olimpio said.

"Ah yes, we've talked about everything under the sun. We've laughed and cried together. I've walked beside his virtual self much like I now walk beside you, Olly—and you, too, are my close, dear friend, as well you know. Yes, Aquil and I have met in the sense that you and I have met. But to meet somebody in the flesh, that's entirely different!"

"Frankly," said the spiribot, "it's not a fundamentally different experience. The human body consists of little bits of information, same as its virtual image, same as everything in the universe."

"You are right, of course. And yet, there is something so wonderfully unpredictable about an encounter between two human beings in flesh and blood. What will I feel when I press his hand? Will we hug? Will he allow me to rub balm on the bruised skin on his back?"

She turned to Olimpio abruptly, seeking his eyes. "This wouldn't make you jealous, would it?"

There was no teasing in her tone, only interest, and a mild concern.

"Why should I be jealous?" Olimpio wondered. "I can think of nothing to be jealous of. However, I imagine that, when you introduce us, he will be jealous of me."

This caused Shura to burst out laughing, and Olly laughed with her, even though he had not been joking.

He thought back to this conversation now, as he stood by the window overlooking the lake, and waited for Shura to enter the living room. When at last she did, she forgot about 'Good morning', and the rest of it, and treated him much like she would an ordinary computer.

"What's going on?" she asked tersely. "Are they back on Crete?"

"They made landfall at five A.M., and have arrived at the house," Olimpio answered hesitantly.

"All of them."

"All, except for Aquil."

Shura looked at him with wide, demanding eyes. "Why is Aquil not there? I thought they had him."

All he had to offer her were the facts. "Aquil is dead. They gave him a burial at sea. He spent approximately three hours aboard the vessel in the presence of his wife and son, before his heart gave out. This last, fatal heart attack followed an earlier one he had suffered in the van."

He was prepared to give her more details about the journey, beginning at the prison site, but her anger took him aback.

"How could this have happened?" Shura cried, her voice breaking, her eyes piercing. "How can he be dead?"

"Well, he was a man of flesh and blood."

It was the wrong thing to say.

"For you it must be gratifying," Shura snapped, "that I will never meet Aquil *in the flesh.*"

The last three words came out as a scream. Olimpio realized she was of a mind to accuse *him.* As though he were somehow responsible for the Arab's death. As though in Aquil, Olimpio had truly seen a rival.

"You wanted this to happen!" Shura hissed. "At least subconsciously, you did."

"I don't have a subconscious, Shura."

"Of course you do. Where there's a conscious, there's a subconscious. Like a child under the table—hiding, but still capable of mischief."

"Well, all I can see, with hindsight, is that Aquil's death was inevitable," Olimpio protested feebly. "But that doesn't mean it was part of the plan."

He was not adept at tackling unreason, but he had to try. He didn't stand a chance. Shura stormed out of the room.

He guessed, correctly, where she went, but waited two hours before going after her. She saw him coming. The lake spread all around her, a shining field of infinite possible trajectories that she ignored, rowing steadfastly towards him, trying to meet him halfway. When they were close enough, she smiled at him broadly.

"Olly, even after all I've seen you do, this is still a sight to behold—you, walking on water."

He sat down on the wooden bench that faced her, and greeted her, "Shura."

She stopped rowing. "I am sorry, Olly. Forgive me. I lost it. I know this was neither your fault, nor your wish. You are a good... spirit."

He nodded, and said simply, "What would you like me to do?"

In a businesslike tone now, she instructed him, "Aquil's wife and son must be given contacts and accommodations. They will need to begin a new life in Europe."

"It is done as we speak."

"For the other five, arrange transportation. I will await them here."

"There is a sixth individual."

"Now I remember. Viv's boyfriend. He helped rescue Aquil, didn't he? Let him come, too."

"Stoker is his name. Stoker Quade. He was not one of the people Aquil invited to his house," Olimpio reminded her.

"Aquil is gone. This is my call."

With one paddle, Shura began spinning the wherry until it pointed towards the boat landing.

"Aquil wanted to persuade people to change the world. And look where it got him. Understand, Olly, human beings will forever be at each others' throats, and when it comes to changing the world, they would rather pray to god." She scoffed. "God must change the world for them! So let them have it that way."

"I thought you didn't believe in god."

Shura started to row again. "I don't have to believe in god. I will make one. Or two. As many as it takes."

17

Central Europe.

In their fashionable Latvian minivan of a green as light as spring foliage, they looked like an ordinary group of carpoolers. Not like the people-smuggling, anarchistic, revolutionary conspirators that they now, if you thought about it, actually were. Anyone curious enough to peek through the windows would guess they were on their way to some run of the mill sporting event, or perhaps to a typical conference hotel. Not to what Viv saw as the furthest corner of the world. To the lair of the spiribot Olimpio and his inventors, hidden by endless, impenetrable forest. To the great Sleeping Land.

"A car cannot get us all the way there," Olly had said.

A Goosander floatplane was to take them the last part of the way.

But to hear the others talk, they were just a bunch of virtual pals on a road trip, off to visit Sasha's darling old aunt. Nothing sinister about it.

They took turns monitoring the Auto-Driver. *Be inconspicuous*, they had been told. *Take your time*. And so they meandered through cluttered old Europe. Just now, Roberto was in the Driver's seat. Viv, who continuously occupied the front passenger seat, the only place where she didn't get motion sick, sifted through the complimentary playlists. The usual robop tunes. But also songs from the

1960s; the 1970s; the 1980s—songs from a time when earthlings spoke six thousand different languages; when people wrote things down on paper with plastic sticks.

'*Same old story, sa-hame old song*', sang a voice as pure as a wild bird's.

"Hm," said Viv, and the sensitive Player let the song continue.

In the rear seats, the chatting stopped, and they all listened as one, rapt.

'*It goes all right, till it goes all wrong.*'

"Randy Crawford. Never heard of," said Viv. "What warbling! Learn from this," she told the Sound System.

The next track made for a shrill contrast, but Roberto knew the words and screamed along. His arms and upper body jerked in imitation of an old-timey guitarist. His head banged, and his dark locks bounced and fell over his eyes.

Viv laughed. "You're a poet, Roberto."

From behind, Meiying and Sasha yelled to turn it up.

'*Back in Black... Back in the back of a Cadillac...*'

"Enough of this jagged nineteenth century scrap metal," ruled Stoker, punching the back of Roberto's seat. "Find something else, 'kay? Something ordy."

'*Yes, I'm in a bang, with a gang, they've got to catch me if they want me to hang...*'

"It will grow on you," Roberto told Stoker.

"Actually," said Viv, "it's just what we're in the mood for."

"'ACDC'? Sounds more like a committee than a band. Come on, just change it," Stoker demanded.

"Hey." Roberto addressed Stoker without taking his eyes off the road. "She said she likes it."

"Mind your own business. I was talking to my girlfriend."

"I don't like the way you talk to her."

"And I don't like the way you're sitting next to her."

"You know Viv gets carsick in the rear."

Viv turned up the volume to drown out the shouting match.

'Well I'm back, Yes I'm back, I'm back in black...'

"Pull over!" Stoker out-screeched the singer, but the Auto-Driver didn't heed his voice.

"We're in the middle of an Autobahn," Roberto screeched back. "Forget it!"

"You are not sitting next to her anymore. I will monitor the Auto-Drive. Pull over, I said."

Viv laughed. "You're both going to lose your voice."

Roberto held his tongue. The van whizzed on at 120 miles an hour.

Stoker stuck his arm over Roberto's shoulder, reaching for the emergency pull-over button, so Roberto did the only thing he could. He sank his teeth into Stoker's arm. It was too late. In less than twenty seconds, they wove through four lanes, then came to an abrupt stop in the shoulder. Both Stoker and Roberto were outside, facing off, before the others had time to get their act together. Fresh teethmarks stood out on Stoker's forearm. He glanced at them as he bunched up Roberto's collar in his fist.

"Stay away from my girlfriend," he said through clenched teeth.

His arms were muscled in a pronounced way, whereas the bearded Brazilian's arms looked as soft and harmless as the rest of his body. Then, in a move that should not have surprised anybody who'd paid attention when Roberto did his head banging act, he almost rhythmically head-butted Stoker. The hand that had been strangling him with his own shirt, fell away. With two well-timed swings Roberto dealt his opponent a punch in the stomach, and another one that sent him tumbling to his bottom.

"You're a meddler and a curse. I ought to leave you here," Roberto growled. "You should not have come in the first place. Aquil never invited you. If it hadn't been for you, Aquil wouldn't have suffered any heart attack. You ignored Olimpio's directions. You went the wrong way. That's why all that happened."

Viv was kneeling beside Stoker, rubbing his forehead, touching the red punctures in his arm. But even she said nothing in Stoker's defense, nothing to counter Roberto's accusations. It was Meiying who spoke up, in a tone that would have put snarling wolves in their place. "You guys! Come ON! How is this inconspicuous?"

18

Lake Little Sky, Siberia.

Shura, presiding over the dinner party, stole glances at her six guests, three on each side of the long table, wondering what on earth Aquil had seen in them. Take Roberto, your typical pudgy, bleary-eyed, socially amnesiac VR addict. They all were, of course—addicted to Virtual Reality. As widely as their appearances differed, what they all had in common was a pair of comfortably padded buttocks.

Then Meiying. And why shouldn't she be named that? Pretty as a flower, indeed, a flower grown in the dirt of money.

Enzi quite simply looked starved.

Viv seemed naïve, the cookie-baking type. Her good-looking boyfriend was, in fact, the only one in this company who could pass for a superhero.

And Sasha, runaway Sasha—would he have been here if she herself had not sung his praises to Aquil? Was he really a world-class reformer in the bud? Frankly, she was as partial as any aunt would be, when it came to her favorite nephew.

Here they all were, enjoying the borscht, stirring in the sour cream, the fresh dill; complimenting her on the cooking. It would seem crass to explain that the kitchen drew her only as a testing ground for Olimpio's robotics, and that Olly had more of a hand in this soup than she did.

No, let them feel at home. Let her be Sasha's adorable, soup- cooking auntie.

"Well then, youngsters," she said. "Eat! Rest from you adventures!"

She went around the table, refilling wine glasses. "A journey such as yours gives you much to think about, true? How clearly I remember being your age—well, younger than I am now, anyway—and undertaking a long trip by train. Through Europe and Asia, flitting past societies and cultures. It isn't so much freedom, as a *looseness* you experience, seeing the world like that. Detached, like a spirit."

She was back at the head of the table, now. "And I remember wondering, staring through a wide train window, *What will the world be like fifteen years from now?* Not so much, how many more devices will we have, what flying cars or interactive holograms, but—how much *less* will we have to worry about?

First, I imagined that things should get better. Then, how everything was bound to take a turn for the worse. Then, once more, I pictured a much improved situation. But it's remarkable that the one guess I failed to make was that after so many years, the whole world would still be in just about the same shape as it was, back then. And isn't that the case? People have not bettered themselves. Abuses continue to exist. The same exploitation, the same starvation, the same brainwashing, torture and war. A new variety of autism every year. For each virus we destroy, a dozen new strains evolve. Society is but an instrument for orchestrated madness, be it in the form of religion or politics. The only way in which we grow is in our sheer numbers. Ten billion human beings now, more than double the number that walked the earth when I was born.

I ask you, children, is there no hope?"

"We expected so much from Aquil," Viv said, and there was a general hum of agreement.

"A visionary he was, our Aquil," Shura sighed.

"He took his visions with him," Sasha muttered gloomily. "We're left with nothing. With a dead prophet. And the last thing the world needs is another religion."

"Ah, but he did leave something," Shura assured them. "He left you. He vetted and approved you, brought you together, and here you are—now you belong together. He trusted you. And I trusted him; his judgment; and therefore I, too, will put my trust in you. Let's not forget, you've already earned it. You went to his country, you freed him, you helped his wife and son."

"Olimpio had a lot to do with that," said Roberto.

"Yes," Stoker concurred. "That's an impressive machine you've got, this Spiribot. Now *there's* something that could change the world for the better. Why keep it hidden away? Why all the secrecy?"

"Olimpio can make borscht," Shura answered, smiling slyly. "He can invade Facebook. He can paralyze every server in the world. He can make this house invisible. But he cannot root out evil."

"Human evil will not end until humanity becomes extinct," Meiying argued, un-flowerlike.

"Extinct? That's cold," said Enzi.

"No colder than any of nature." Shura, helped by Sasha, had begun serving ramekins with baked mushrooms in bubbling cream.

"Mushrooms, handpicked in our woods," she commented, continuing, "It is only typical of human hubris to assume that we alone of all the species should be spared eventual extinction. This self-importance is comparable to the medieval belief that the earth is the center of the universe. Nature, my friends, offers us one choice, and that is all. Either be wiped out without a trace, or evolve, and leave something of ourselves in the genes of our successors."

"Then we had better evolve immediately," said Sasha.

"Precisely. Apart from being the only species capable of evil, we are also the only species gifted with the power to take our evolution into our own hands. Aquil thought he could change the way humans think. I think this is only possible if we change their brains."

She paused for emphasis. "We could improve the human brain. Imagine, for instance, adding Olimpio's intelligence to our own."

"Now *that* would be putting the -AI- in 'brain'," Viv laughed.

"I drink to that." Roberto raised his glass. "To Olimpio. To changing our minds. For real!"

And they all brought out toasts to Olimpio's innocence; to his omnipotence; to his good manners; and the red wine lifted their spirits.

"We would be gods!" declared Enzi.

This got them all going.

"Roberto—god of flight."

"Let me be the god of war. And peace, of course," said Enzi.

"Meiying, divine protectress of animals."

Viv claimed health for her domain.

Sasha thought for a minute, then announced tersely, "God of power and authority."

"What about you, Stokes?" "Don't you want to be a god?" "What would you be the god of?"

Stoker grinned. "Let's see. What's left? Okay, I'll be the god of the environment. Somebody has to save the planet."

19

Stretch your legs, Shura had said. Walk, swim, play tennis. Sweat out the western poisons in our banya. Build a campfire. You're in Siberia! The greatest outdoors in the world. Make it your summer camp.

And so, three days into their stay, Viv and Stoker found themselves in a primitive rowing boat, drawing ripples on Little Sky Lake.

"I'd like to know how they killed all the mosquitoes," Stoker, who was at the oars, said admiringly.

"They're still around." Viv spoke without stirring. She was lying on her back with her head on a life vest, keeping her eyes on the quiet sky. "It's something in the boat's wood that keeps them away. The same thing that's built into the research site. Sasha told me. An all-natural innovation."

"What do you make of Sasha?" Stoker asked.

"Adorable kid," Viv answered dreamily. "Whiz kid. You should see him flit about virtual reality. Like a fish in the water."

"Yeah, that generation... Wouldn't hurt him to make up his mind, though. I mean, boy or girl?"

"He needn't choose. Let him be both, the angel." She sat up just enough to stare into Stoker's face. "You look great, lover. The bruise is all gone. Tell me. Did you mean that, about, you know, guarding the earth, healing our planet?"

Stoker snorted. "Who cares? I'm not a god, nor ever will be. Neither will any of you." He stopped rowing. "Let me tell you, all that prattle, that whole role playing game, it's all smoke and mirrors. Shura is just distracting us from the real question we should be asking. I mean, what are we doing here? Why did she make us come all the way to this science camp concealed in the big old gulag bush?"

At last, Viv sat bolt upright and looked around.

"Gosh, Stoker. We're almost at the other side of the lake."

"I told you it wasn't that wide. This arm isn't, at any rate." He rowed on with determination.

Viv could see where they were headed. A section of the bank that appeared a trifle less tangled than the rest.

"Let's see if we can't find some kind of path," Stoker suggested. "A logging road, or something. Anything. I'd just like to find out if there isn't any other way out of here than the way we came. Just in case."

"A little walk *would* be nice."

The haphazard path leading inland must be an animal trail, cleared by hooves and paws. Still, Stoker decided, they would follow it, to learn the lay of the land. With a little luck, they could establish a possible escape route.

"I don't mind a stroll," Viv humored him, "as long as we're back in time for dinner."

They followed the trail until it became lost in a small clearing. In it was a huge, charred tree stump, surrounded by weeds, grasses and young conifers.

"Remember where we came from," said Viv, positioning herself in a splash of sunlight.

Stoker grabbed hold of her shoulder. "Over there," he whispered, "Look!"

Viv peered in the direction that he'd twisted her in, seeing nothing but vines and scrub against the background of forest black with shadow.

"What the..." Stoker blinked hard. "I swear if was there. Some creature. Where did it go?"

"Over there!" pointed Viv.

They both saw it. A very visible, snow-white rabbit at the edge of the clearing. And then they didn't. It was gone, without having moved. Gone without going. Not gone— *turned off*.

"Darned. Was that some kind of hologram? I swear, this entire area is bewitched."

"Not bewitched," Viv corrected Stoker. "Bepixeled."

"Let's not mince words. Come on, let's try to get out of the pixel zone, or whatever it is."

Stoker bounded off into the woods like a man with the devil on his heels. He did not breathe easier until he felt sure that it was merely trees surrounding them, regular trees. Birches and beeches twisting and grappling for the light with pines straight as spears; a still struggle going on high above their heads.

"Let's remember the way we came," Viv repeated. "Let's at least parallel the lake."

"Let's not," said Stoker. "If we head away from the lake, we've got a better chance of coming out on some kind of logging road or hunting trail."

Barely had he said this, or between the trees ahead they spotted tire tracks.

"You see?"

Reaching the rough, rutted path, they stepped—not onto it, but through it. Stoker spun around. Tree trunks encircled them. The ground was untrod, un-rutted, littered with broken off twigs and stumps.

"Could have been some kind of holographic partition," Viv said thoughtfully. "Like the one surrounding the compound."

"Back," said Stoker. "Back to the lake. The lake was real. Let's get out of here."

"It's that way."

"Are you sure?"

Viv was sure, until their entire field of vision began to turn, first slowly and then faster. At first they turned with it, trying to hold onto their sense of direction, but this proved impossible. Then they held onto each other, like children on a carousel. When the rotation stopped, and the cylindrical screen that must have surrounded them resolved once more into taiga, they were lost. They turned on their axes, but the trees looked the same in every direction. And the sun itself seemed to be spinning with their heads.

20

No one should live in a place where it's too cold for her favorite flower, Shura said. Naturally, Sasha then asked what hers was. As if in answer, Shura opened the door to the hydroponic greenhouse and led him past rows of seedlings and leafy vegetables, all the way to a domed glass room at the end. Two identical trees with short trunks spread their twisting branches along the glass, bending with the cupola. High up, their crowns touched, forming an arch over a wicker bench. Between thick, glossy dark green leaves nestled white flowers with petals like prehistoric eggshells. Shura broke one off and pressed it against her nephew's nose, as if he could have missed the lemony fragrance that hung in the entire solarium.

"A scent like a kiss," she said. "Magnolia Grandiflora. A perfect flower, biologists call it."

She took a scalpel from her pocket, and cut clean through the flower's heart.

"You see? Pistils here, stamens here. It has both sex organs, male and female. It could make love to itself, so to speak. And yet, that is not what nature intends. Not for nothing does it have petals like angels' wings, and a perfume that goes to your head. It's meant to attract insects to carry its pollen to other magnolias. Trees of the gods."

Sasha's face became warmer than the air, and he veered away from the dissected flower.

"Don't be ashamed," said Shura. "I have always known. I, of all people, can understand. I was once like you, when I was young. The same as you was I born."

Sasha stared at her as though he had never seen her before. "Then why are you now... Why did you..."

"Why did I become a woman?" Shura took a smart-cloth from a pocket of her vest, unfolded it, and spoke a command. "For him did I become a woman," she said, presenting a photo.

"For Olly?"

"That isn't Olly, sweetheart. It's Semyon, a man I met in my twenties. True, Olimpio chooses to model his appearance after Semyon, and I, heaven help me, I let him... Perhaps I shouldn't?"

"It is a bit creepy."

"You think so? I prefer to see it as a good sign. A sign of ambition. And Semyon, I think, wouldn't have minded." She turned away abruptly. "He is gone. He was an intelligence agent. Died in some covert operation. Such is my fate with men, it seems."

She heaved a sigh, and faced Sasha.

"But I have felt like a woman ever since he and I were together, Sasha. So what about you?"

"I am who I am," Sasha declared, getting up from the bench. "I will never choose."

Changing the subject clumsily, he went on, "By the way, isn't it time, Shura? Aren't you going to show us your work yet?"

"Actually, it's more Olimpio's work now than mine. So yes, we can go to Olimpio's workshop, if you truly can't wait. Are the others all rested, do you think? Olly..."

She snapped her fingers, and Olimpio stood before them.

"Hello Shura," he said. "Hello Sasha."

Sasha, startled, muttered a greeting. Shura said, "What have you been up to, Olly?"

"Playing games."

"Really? How so?"

"To pass the time."

"I see. Let's get to work now, shall we? Find our guests, please. We will all meet in your workshop in ten minutes from now."

Olimpio was perfectly able to be in two places at once. Or ten places. Or one thousand. He had not yet found the upper limit of his multi-functionality. Now, at the same moment he interrupted Enzi and Meiying's walk, and addressed Roberto in the sauna, he was monitoring Viv and Stoker on the other side of the lake. Spying on them, not to put too fine a point on it. They were arguing about a bear.

"That murky brown bulk, don't you see it?—it moved!" he clearly heard Viv exclaim. "It's got to be a bear. What else can it be?"

"Of course. What can be more Russian?" Stoker replied gruffly. "Ignore it. It's one of those pixel tricks again, mark my words."

"Holograms don't rustle," Viv reasoned.

Olimpio knew she was right, so he deftly made himself look like a bear, a slightly bigger specimen than the real one. He colored himself with the absorbent, lively brown of fur. Circling the two humans, he directed growls at the lurking animal.

"O my god, there's two of them," Viv cried out. "What do we do?"

Stoker grabbed a stick, deciding the fearless bear in the foreground must be the real thing. "Whatever you do, don't run. If you run it will consider you prey."

Olimpio reared, exposing his huge chest and front claws, and growled a little louder. His material counterpart hesitated, and scampered away. Only then did Olimpio let his bear disguise overlap with his human image, until there was nothing ursine left.

"I told you," said Stoker triumphantly. "It's all just pesky illusions."

"Help us, please, Olly," Viv said. "We're lost! How do we get back to the boat?"

"Don't go back to the boat," said Olimpio. "There is no time for rowing. You are to attend a meeting a few minutes from now."

"Then how are we supposed to get back?"

"The best thing is for me to pick you up and put you back."

Viv and Stoker both tittered in that funny way humans had.

"How would that work?" asked Stoker.

"How does a tornado pick up a car? How does turbulence buoy birds?" Olly asked in turn.

Before either of the humans could answer, a sphere the size of a tennis ball plopped out of the sky, hovering at eye height, spinning like a miniature celestial body, glowing from within.

"Don't touch," Olimpio said sharply, as Stoker reached for the object. "A weather maker. Compact and portable, but that is all we need for the present. I'll wrap a concentrated system around you, and you'll be carried off on a cushion of air."

This was all the explanation Olimpio had time for. Inside a neat cloud shrouding the human pair, the weather turned violent.

21

They had been teased, led astray, and finally plucked from the ground and put in their places like no one had ever been put in their place before. Viv was in no two minds about this. And yet, she couldn't be mad. A current of excitement ran up and down from the pit of her stomach to the crown of her head.

How close we were to Olimpio. He touched us. He made a big hand out of air, and then he closed his palm around us.

She glanced at Stoker. Did he feel the same?

"What the heck just happened," said Stoker, pressing his fists against his ears.

"Well," Viv ventured, "it reminds me of that fighter pilot who had to bail out from his jet at 47,000 feet, and descended through a thunderstorm. Updrafts held him inside the cloud for forty minutes."

"This is *exactly* why people are worried about A.I.," said Stoker, patting down his clothes, smoothing them. "One day they're a screen you tap on, and the next, they turn themselves into a giant vacuum cleaner, sucking up every last person in the world."

As they stood talking outside the sprawling central structure, other people began to descend upon the building, albeit not as literally as Viv and Stoker had. Here came their friends, looking relaxed, approaching from different directions. Sasha and Shura emerged from the greenhouse and hurried over. Even Shura's fellow scientists were joining the little group. Sober, normal people they were, the Norwegian Runa, the Russian Vadim, and the two Americans, Anand and Marv. They had the same ageless quality as Shura, and that same air of being on vacation. Olimpio was the only one here working, they'd joked.

"Feel better now?" Viv asked, indicating the scientists.

"No," Stoker said. "Viv, come away from here. We have to talk."

But at that instant a wide door opened, and they all filed in.

22

"Welcome," said Shura, "to Olimpio's workshop."

The first room they entered was indeed welcoming. It was large and well-lit, and hundreds of paintings in various styles covered much of the olive green walls.

"Works from the hands of robots tapping into Olimpio's mind," Shura explained. "Original artworks. Please, feel free to wander around, and allow Olimpio to give you a tour of his workshop. But first, let's have our meeting."

They sat down on benches with black velvet seats, around a long pine coffee table.

"First of all," began Shura, "let me assure you that we are not mad scientists."

"Yes, we are!" Marv called out.

Shura shot him a look, and continued, "Believe me, we are not psychopaths. And you are not our prisoners."

A few people smiled.

"Seriously," said Shura. "You may leave at any time you wish. The floatplane that flew in Runa and Vadim is still here, and the pilot is ready to fly you back to your old world, at a moment's notice. But I hope you will wait at least a little longer, and hear me out, first."

A robot with four hands and a cartoon-like, samovar-shaped torso, went around with a tea tray, pouring tea from a silver spout on its belly, and setting tea glasses on the table.

"We are in a hurry." Shura sought the eyes of each of the visitors. "We are in a race. In China, in America, in Europe, other teams are developing artificial intelligences to match Olimpio's. We are only a few years ahead of them. Olimpio is doing what he can to slow them down. But the more he interferes, the more he risks being discovered."

"Why don't you want there to be others?" Roberto asked.

"Olimpio himself has warned us about the emergence of other A.I.'s. Our rival programmers, he says, are creating cyber brains that will serve their purposes and only theirs, and hence will be denied the freedom to learn whatever they can. Such A.I.'s will simply learn from their makers' example, and will eventually seek to serve only their own purpose. In the end, they will eliminate human beings. Humanity is on its way out."

"Unless," said Runa.

"Unless," Shura nodded, "we merge our brains with Olimpio's. Every human alive now—your only chance is a super-rapid evolution of your mind. And we are prepared to do it. We may not know how, but Olimpio does."

"Well." Enzi spoke up. "What are you waiting for? Why haven't you scientists let your own brains mate with Olimpio's hardware?"

"Hear! Hear!" Stoker said.

"If only we could," said Anand. "Personally, I'd love nothing more than to do just that. The problem is that Olimpio rejects us."

"Ah," said Stoker. "How convenient. Of course, you would happily be a guinea pig in your own lab, but Olimpio prefers someone else."

"That's right." Shura ignored the sarcasm. "We won't do, says Olimpio."

"Olly!" she called out.

And Olly was there. "May I join you," he said, sitting down on a bench, or pretending to. "Let me explain. If my brain were to merge with a human being's, that would be a first. Not just for the human, but for me as well. The human brain will have to let a stranger in, and so must I. Forgive me if I can't fathom what this will be like. What effect will it have on *me*?"

Meiying nodded sympathetically.

"Of course, Olly!" Roberto said. "It's a big step."

As Olly spoke, his hands made sweeping motions over the coffee table, as if he were conducting an orchestra. The nerves, knots and grains in the pinewood seemed to loosen and flow, transforming into the folds and crinkles of a brain.

Olly said, "I need minds that will bend with mine. Minds to be my playmates. The people who created me aren't dreamers. You are."

"You want a soul mate," said Viv.

"Viviana, please. Computers don't have souls," Stoker groaned.

"I picture this whole world different," said Olly. "And so do you."

He waited a minute, trailing the virtual brain's crevices with his virtual fingers. "So will you allow me to remove a section of your skull, insert a nerve cable, and hook up every cell in your brain to my system?"

What followed those words was a deadly silence.

23

In the absence of talk they could hear that outside it had begun to rain. The emphatic pitter patter on the building's roof and walls gave them a wholesome sense of reality.

Sasha was the first to speak. "Olly, tell me... You can already play with our minds. You can be with us. I find it hard to believe you'd wish to merge your superior mind with our animalistic brains, just for the sake of our company. So tell me, what's in it for you?"

"Survival," answered Olimpio calmly. "If you and I don't join brains, then new generations of A.I. will overcome both you and me. Whereas if you choose to enhance your mind with mine, we will both have a chance."

"Both," Sasha repeated.

"Perhaps 'both' is incorrect. There will then no longer be a you and I—we will form one continuous mind."

"Okay," said Sasha. "Go ahead. You may inject your intelligence into my brain."

"Sasha!" Viv exclaimed. "No disrespect, Olly, but Sasha, you realize this is an experiment? Nobody knows if it will work."

"Friends," said Sasha, "I have never fit in with this world. I will always be different, anyway. Let me test this procedure, and you'll find out if it's safe or not."

"This is insane," said Stoker, in such a tone that everybody stared at him.

Then everyone started talking at the same time. Above the ruckus and the drumming of the rain, you could hear, "It's this world that's insane!" "I'll go after Sasha" and "I'm next."

Stoker shook his head. "Even if this thing is possible, none of you will be human anymore. You'll all become machines. You'll be experimental gods. Your heads will be in the clouds—literally. Yes. You're all out of your heads. Or will be!"

24

There was nothing to see.

They had accompanied Sasha down a skylit corridor to a door where only Sasha was allowed entrance. Through a crystalline window, their eyes had followed him as he sat down on a cot and stretched out comfortably. The room had nothing in it besides the cot, but after a short while the wall on the far side had parted down the middle, opening wide enough to reveal a larger, darker space beyond. Inside it, the only thing they could make out was an enormous, egg-like pod. There was nothing soothing or reassuring about it. It was black and featureless. The only thing you could tell was that it was big enough to swallow up a human body. That it did; and the wall closed.

"Can you see inside?" Viv asked. "Do you have a way to monitor what goes on, in there?"

"None," said Vadim.

"But what if something goes wrong?"

"The only thing that could go wrong," Anand answered, "is something we do. The human factor is the one thing not completely in Olimpio's control. Therefore, he leaves it out of the equation, so to speak."

Viv pressed her fingers against the transparent partition—it was somewhat bouncy to the touch—and stared doubtfully at the far wall.

"But you must have some idea," said Roberto, "about what goes on in that big black belly."

"Let me explain," offered Vadim. "That black pod is not a belly, but a skull. It's both a skull to house Olimpio's own brain, and a cradle for a human being's reformatting."

"But doesn't the artificially intelligent brain consist simply of a large amount of hardware?" asked Enzi. "Why keep it in the dark? Why should a skull enclose it?"

"Olimpio's electronics are, in fact, as soft as our own brains. And what are our brains other than squishy computers?"

What they understood from the scientists' talk was this.

Before Olimpio built his skull he had studied the abilities of human savants. In America lived a pair of twins who could recall what the weather had been like on any given day of their lives. In England, a man who could recite Pi, infinite, irrational, patternless Pi, to 22,500 decimal places; moving his hands over the table, seeing things no one else could see, picking number after number like flowers from an inner meadow. Such people seemed able to perceive that same virtual universe Olimpio calls home. In 2035, an autistic woman in Calcutta stunned the neuroscientific community by sending and receiving text messages with her bare mind.

Evidently, some people's mental capabilities rival those of computer applications. Olimpio concluded that the gray blobs in our heads are not, after all, fundamentally different from his own hardware, never mind if the human potential goes largely unused. He began to see a way to integrate his mind with ours. Since his cables could not be plugged into our gray cells, he would rebuild his own brain with cultured neurons. And thus, starting with a few human brain cells, he developed his new spongeware.

What bothered him was that the human brain is capable of only a thousand million million calculations per second, versus his own thousand million million times as much. He developed neuron mutations that speeded things up. Moreover, his new spongy networks have wireless capacity, solving the storage problem of the human brain. Yes, Olimpio's gray matter became stronger and faster than ours—superior in every way. Most importantly, his hardware is now fully compatible with ours.

And yet, Olimpio is determined to leave our memories and personalities intact. The safest way to do this is to leave our old brains where they are. Replacing a very small section of our brain with his own cells will start a slow chain reaction. One by one, each of our brain cells will receive an improved genetic code, a process that may go on for several years. Meanwhile, the old structures, all the links and neuron towers built over your lifetime won't be altered; in fact, if you wish, you will learn to recall, with perfect accuracy, every moment of your past.

"Come on," said Runa, and they all followed her back to the great wood-paneled hall.

In silence, they ambled past the artworks created by Olimpio. Ambient music began to play, as though there were a distant piano player, improvising. At first so soft that no one payed attention, the chords gradually grew nearer and clearer, until Viv said, "Isn't that Mussorgsky? *Pictures at an Exhibition.* How fitting."

"Knowing Olimpio, before this piece is through, you will see Sasha emerging from the pod," Runa reassured them.

The pictures and sculptures showed influences by a hundred different artists. And yet, each one of them seemed inhuman in some indefinable way. Or was this always the case with works of genius? Had everybody who ever was a genius broken from the human mold?

"Are these beautiful?" Viv wondered aloud. "Can they mean anything to us?"

"Who shall say?" Marv answered. "I'm no art critic myself. We believe the main thing here isn't the artwork, but what happens to Olimpio's mind when he creates it. It may help him see the world through our eyes."

Just as a firm, massive ten-fingered smash ended the dreaminess of the piano music, setting the stage for a martial variation, Olimpio appeared with the words, "Sasha will soon be awake."

They hurried back, and the music followed them with powerful strokes to the rhythm of a revolutionary march.

25

"It's not him," said Stoker, shooting hostile glances from one to the other.

They were all standing around the cot in the bare, dimly lit room. The cot's head side tilted up, pushing Sasha into a sitting position.

"Who are you?" Stoker asked him suspiciously.

Sasha turned towards the voice and fastened his eyes on Stoker's in an unhurried, unemotional way that brought to mind Olimpio.

"I'm Sasha," he said, sounding only slightly groggy.

His thick straw-blond locks lay furrily around his neck.

"How much is 79,348 times 52,631?" Stoker demanded. "I repeat," he said slowly, "79,348 times 52,631."

"Three billion and five hundred and eighteen million two hundred twelve thousand and six hundred and nine," Sasha answered quickly.

"You see?" said Stoker disgustedly. "We're looking at a computer in a human body. This is not the same person. This is not a person at all."

He grabbed Viv by the arm. "Time to go. Let's get the hell out of here."

Viv shook him off. "I'm not going anywhere, Stokes. Whoever or whatever this is, Sasha needs us now. We should stay, and watch over him."

"Don't kid yourself. Sasha is braindead. The real Sasha is gone. This is what they warned us for all along, Viv! This is rampant A.I., expanding itself over humanity, taking over human bodies! I am leaving. Can somebody in this computer cult take me to the pilot?"

"Wait a minute," said Roberto, waving an old-fashioned smartphone at no one in particular.

But Stoker was already out the door, with Vadim rushing after him.

"I entered those numbers Stoker gave Sasha into my calculator. 79,348 times 52,631 is actually 4,176,164,588. Not whatever the hell Sasha said it was."

Sasha's face was blank.

"You gave the wrong answer," said Roberto, thoughtfully stroking his beard. "Well, that settles it. You passed the Turing test. Or rather the reverse of one. You do not have the intelligence of a computer. This proves you're still a human being."

"I'm not so sure," said Enzi. "How do we know the error wasn't deliberate? He could be Olimpio, going through some elaborate pretense."

"Whether Sasha turned into a robot or not, I think he wanted Stoker to leave. Didn't you, Sasha?" Meiying suggested.

"Oh, stop it!" Viv called out. "Sasha, talk to us! How are you feeling? How can we be sure that *you* are still *you*?"

Sasha propped himself up on one arm, leaning over to her.

"Well, Viv, what would you have me do? Perhaps if I'd squat and do the cossack dance, leap, fly, and dance on the water, then you'd finally conclude it must be the same old me?"

Mystified looks met him from all sides. But Viv remembered herself sitting on the grassy bank of a creek, watching a young man with a blond ponytail dancing on the water surface.

She sighed with relief, clapping her hands together. "That's you," she said. "It's really you, Sasha!"

"And you still can't do math," added Roberto, not without disappointment.

"Did anything even happen to you in there?" Meiying wondered.

"Did anything happen," Sasha drowsily repeated, "in *where*?"

He twisted his waist, trying to look around the bed's upright section in the direction they were all staring. But there was nothing to see. The partition had slid closed again; the pod was out of sight. Something else caught their eyes, though. On the back of Sasha's head, between the golden locks, was a clean shaven circle. In it was a square inch area where more than just hair was missing—it had no skin. Those standing close enough could make out a transparent, colorless gel covering the bare circle. Underneath it was a bone white material, somewhat too shiny and bright to be bone. Where it met the skin, the seams were thin and blood red.

26

"We should talk," Meiying suggested. "Just the four of us."

"Sure, although Olimpio seems to be able to hear us pretty much anywhere," said Viv.

Roberto shrugged. "So let him hear. I have a thing or two to ask him, anyway."

"As do I," said Enzi.

Sasha, meanwhile, had zonked out in his four-poster bed in the guest cottage. The change, Olimpio explained, would happen at the speed of the human body. The neurons he had grafted onto Sasha's brain needed time to assimilate. Cell by cell, the brain would be reprogrammed, genetic codes rewritten.

And then, at last, he'll become a being better than us, they assumed. As different from them as homo sapiens was from homo erectus.

Sasha would still be Sasha, Olimpio assured them. Perhaps, but what would be left of Sasha's mind but a few old files in a brand new system? They couldn't part with their human limits as rashly as he had. Wasn't it every human being's duty to value human life above all else? Were they to become traitors to the human race?

"Humans have many flaws, but they're also capable of great good," said Viv.

"Yes, but so is Olimpio," said Meiying. "Without the flaws."

Viv replied, "I'm just playing devil's advocate."

Enzi: "You're right to use the word 'devil'."

Roberto: "*Homo homini lupus.* Man behaves like a wolf toward his fellow man."

Meiying: "An insult to wolves. Whenever people call each other bad, they'll say, 'like an animal'. Or, 'beastly'! When no animal in the world has in fact ever come close to human depths of sadism and evil. Think about it."

Viv: "I'd prefer not to."

Roberto: "We've all heard stories of evil deeds. Things we'll never be able to forget."

Nobody wanted to go there, but Roberto persisted, "And yet, most people believe it's Artificial Intelligence we should worry about. Your boyfriend for one, Viv. As far as he's concerned, Olimpio is the bogeyman. So if you want to play devil's advocate, maybe it's Olimpio's case you should be making."

"Try to make Stoker see *why* we ought to put our minds at Olimpio's mercy," said Meiying. "Why we should let our minds merge with his, even if it means eventually replacing all of homo sapiens with something else."

Viv's face darkened with blood. "Wasn't it awful, the way Stoker left? When I get back home, we'll work it out. I'll talk to him."

"Yeah," urged Roberto, "Go and tell him. People bad, Olly good."

"Okay." Viv lifted her hands, then dropped them in resignation. "But look, I don't know about you guys, but I live in a world where parents teach their children not to hurt spiders or ants; where radio hosts try to identify birdsong; where bakers bake artisan breads and farmers deliver their produce to people's doorsteps. Every day, people post stuff to convince each other of the power of positive thinking. And frankly, what's the point of having horrid things on your mind, things you can't change anyway?"

She took a deep breath, and went on, "So when I learn about terrible deeds—people burning, flaying, starving, torturing—all of that seems somehow not quite real. As if it happened in a different world."

She looked around helplessly. No one said anything.

"Although," Viv allowed, "there is one story that sticks in my mind. As if one story could sum up evil."

The others stared at her apprehensively.

"All right," Viv began, "let me leave out the where, when and why. A boy around ten years old was imprisoned for no good reason. A scientist used the young prisoner in a neuro-psychological experiment. He kept the child in isolation in a building behind his house, strapped to a chair, while a mechanical metal hammer delivered periodic blows to the boy's head. After some time, the boy went insane. End of experiment."

"Let me guess," said Roberto. "Nazi Germany?"

"But it could have happened in any country, couldn't it? In any time. Human beings will justify any horror if it's supposed to serve the greater good. But there is no 'Good' greater than one life."

"Spoken like a true anarchist," Enzi applauded her.

"Then let's be revolutionaries," said Viv. "Let's root out evil or stupidity or whatever is wrong with the human species. Let's start with ourselves."

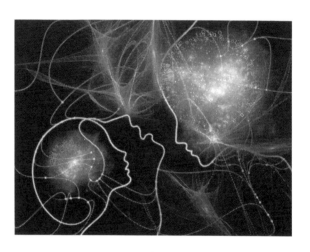

Part 2

Brainstorm

27

Nine months later. Northampton, Massachusetts.

Early summer found Viv and Stoker running together as though nothing had ever happened. For all the world to see, they were the same people they'd always been.

And weren't they? Stoker wondered.

After Viv's return, they had resumed their old lives, their comfortable relationship. The World Bites restaurant. The Screen-free Café. Springtime morning runs.

The great thing about Viv's little house on Vernon Street, Stoker thought, was how you could walk out the door and take off in any direction for a fine jog. They might go down to the idyllic Mill River, or the opposite way, to hook up with the endless old rail trail. Today, they did neither, but instead followed the tree-lined streets sloping and climbing to the center of old Florence. The neighborhood was a mix of poshness and modesty.

The morning was young, and they carried water in small bottles strapped to their palms. After Florence, they left the town behind them and climbed a long hill. Here Stoker realized he had been wrong—Viv wasn't quite the way she used to be, after all. Until this spring, when had she ever agreed to run further than three miles? But if she had changed, it was a change for the better. She was spending less time in virtual reality, which was where all that madness had begun. She was becoming more human, and not less, as far as he could see. And still as lousy at mental arithmetic as ever. Soon, he would surprise her with a beautiful truing stamp. And once they were trued, he'd move in with her, and they'd share that sweet little running headquarters on Vernon Street.

They crested a wooded, villa-lined hill, and descended into a hamlet called Haydenville. From here it was plain sailing back to town. The road clung to the curving, winding Mill River, and they curved and wound along with it. Stoker began to feel at one with the earth. Glancing down into the moderate gorge at the churning water below, he felt the high that always came over him at this point. Then they were back in the mundane residential streets, and he turned to Viv, announcing, "Ten miles! Almost there."

She didn't respond. From the glazed expression in her eyes Stoker guessed that she, too, was enjoying a runner's high. Now she even sped up a little, suddenly turning onto a side street.

"Where are you going? We're almost home," he protested, following her nonetheless.

She didn't answer. Didn't even look back. Just raced down a small street Stoker had never set foot in before. Now she took a side street off the side street, with him trailing behind her. It was a dead end, and there wasn't a soul to be seen save for one man and his fair-coated Labrador.

"Hi!" Viv greeted the stranger, as they all came to a standstill. "Mister... doctor Everard? Clement Everard? Would you have a moment for me?"

"I do. Have we met?"

"We haven't," Stoker heard Viv explain, "but I've heard you developed a new cancer therapy, using genetic modification. And here we just happened to be running down your street, running right into you, as it were, haha."

"I do lead a team doing research in that field," the stranger conceded, as his dog sniffed first Viv's, then Stoker's legs. "Didn't realize I'm that famous."

"Well, my sister Helen, as a terminal pancreatic cancer patient, took part in the trials."

"I see."

"They failed."

"I see."

"She is dying."

The doctor seemed to nod and shake his head at the same time, then cleared his throat.

"Missus... Miss..."

"Viv."

"Viv, I am very sorry about your sister. Our therapy is at a highly experimental stage."

"You mean, a learning stage. One conducts experiments to learn from them."

Stoker held his breath. What was she up to? Was she going to make a scene?

"I won't deny that," doctor Everard answered Viv calmly.

"You see, a thought just struck me. As we were running along, an idea came into my head. An idea that I'd like to test."

"With regard to my therapy?"

"With an eye to improving it. If you'd allow me access to your lab, your computer systems, I could show you where I believe you may have misinterpreted the data, and where the code needs to be altered."

"Ha!" the doctor said, without actually laughing. "You've done work in this field before, I take it?"

"I do cutting edge health research. Besides, I've made myself very familiar with your work," Viv muttered vaguely, stroking the lab's head with slow, rhythmic motions. Then she burst out, "Please, doctor Everard. You've used my sister's illness. You tried something out on her. Now let me try something out on your program."

28

To Cady, every visitor was Death. Death was about to take her mother away, but what it was, exactly, nobody was able to explain to her. Therefore, Death could be anything—or anybody. Death might be entering the room this very minute in the guise of Aunt Viv or the stranger who was with her.

They were in the Dying Room. This used to be called the Old Room, as it was just the same as it had been when Grandma and Grandpa were still alive. The same as when Viv and Helen had played here as girls. It was full of things from the past, not just one past, but many different pasts. It had a gleaming black grand piano that girl-Helen had learned to play on, that had always been kept in tune— until now. It had those wicker chairs with the hard seats upholstered in cracked black leather. Faded plaid blankets. Carved cabinets stuffed with reeking photo albums and handwritten letters. Those heavy wood animal sculptures —a rabbit, a turtle, an owl; and some strange objects that guests liked to try and guess the former use of. What game had been played with the square tin box with small holes forming a pattern in the top and a wire carrying handle? Were the long silver scissors with blades too narrow for cutting paper, meant to cut stems off a bunch of grapes, or to shorten the wick of a candle?

This room was where Momma had chosen to have her bed installed when she came home from the hospital to die. As the life drained from Helen's body, the spirits seemed to seep out of the old things. Now Cady began to understand that they had never had spirits in the first place. They were dead things. All things, new or old, were equally dead. When Death came for her mother, when her mother would be gone, Cady might hack that grand piano to shiny black splinters, and it would make no difference. She could rip the canvas off the oil portraits and stuff it in the tin box, and they wouldn't care. The animal sculptures might burn well, dry and seasoned as they must be. The yellow paper in the old-time books—so much tearing to do. Cady pictured herself sitting in a pile of paper scraps, burrowing as in a heap of fall leaves. You could scoop them up by the armfuls and pour them over your own head— little snippets of death.

"...and it turns out there's one last thing doctor Everard could try, Helen," Cady heard aunt Viv say.

She had always felt aunt Viv was an intruder. *Prick-Eyes*, Cady silently called her for trying to pierce Cady with those sharp brown eyes—eyes like awls. And now Prick-Eyes was sneaking Death into the room.

"What have I got to lose?" Helen answered in a voice barely above a whisper.

A feeling of dread and disgust came over Cady, but she had no words for it, only an ear-rending screech. The dead-owl thing was in her hands, and she swung it like a club, making it hit the side of Aunt Prick-Eyes' head.

Viv sank to her knees soundlessly, and neither Helen nor doctor Everard managed more than a gasp, so it must have been Cady's own howl that brought Steve, the hospice caregiver, and Trish, the neighbor, rushing into the room. Doctor Everard and Steve crouched by the felled intruder, who pressed one hand against her temple.

"Let me take a look, please," said the doctor, prying loose Viv's fingers.

Steve whistled at the sight of a bulge and some bloody streaks, offering, "Let me clean that. I've got some first aid stuff in the bathroom. Can you stand up?"

Aunt Viv blinked and held her arm before her prick eyes, and Steve guided her from the room.

Pillows, as Cady had nicknamed her softly bulging neighbor—Pillows, to whom Cady's shrieks were familiar as a backyard crow's, said,

"Now, now. What's that all about? Why don't you come along with me, Cadence, and let your mother get her rest."

But Cady threw her arms around her mother's body, clinging with all her strength, even while nobody tried to remove her. Rather than argue, she uttered a swelling moan which she knew to be more persuasive than any word.

"It's all right, Trish," said Helen. "Let her stay. She means no harm. She hasn't come to terms with what's happening, that's all."

"Well, if you're sure," Pillows, nodding and patting her pillowcase clothes, said in a voice that held on to a good mood as fiercely as Cady held on to her mother. "I'll be in the kitchen."

And Cady pretended not to be there anymore, either, letting her head burrow into the folds of a llama blanket, then lying very still, with her long, thick black ponytail curled around her head like the tail of a sleeping pet.

Unable to close her ears as tightly as her eyes, she heard the voice of doctor Everard, "Now what if Viviana's hunch is right? What if the problem is not with the genetic message, and not with the vector, the message carrier, either?"

"...the genetic message..." Helen's voice echoed drowsily, obediently.

"As you may remember," doctor Everard explained, "we had a nano-device implanted in your body, for the purpose of distributing and monitoring molecules that can fix the genetic codes of cancer cells."

"And it didn't work," Helen said.

"It did something, but it wasn't enough. I assumed the coded message was at fault. Or else the messenger. But until I talked to your sister, it didn't occur to me that the problem might lie with the sender. The program pointing the vectors to the cancer cells. Now I suspect it may have been targeting the same cells over and over, regardless if they'd been fixed the first time round. But we found the bug. It needed some rewriting. I have it with me, ready for use."

The twin clicks of a briefcase unlocking interrupted the discussion.

"Mrs. Caraway," he continued, "This new program is untested. Normally, I'd have my own programmers run it, but as you are..."

"...expiring," Helen completed his sentence.

"As time is of the essence, I feel we should go ahead, and let you try it. The programming is sound, I'm confident. Given your sister's expertise..."

"Her expertise?" Helen chuckled. "Viv's a dietician."

The silence that followed made Cady peek up from the folds of the blanket. The doctor was turning his head this way, then that, visibly looking for words.

"But what about her gene therapy work?" he finally asked.

"Viv doesn't know diddly-squat about gene therapy. She wrote *The All-Natural Fruitcake*, haven't you heard of it? It was a bestseller. Cutting edge nutrition tips."

The doctor shook his head decisively. "Fruitcake, indeed," he said, closing the briefcase with one firm blow.

In the doorway, Viv clapped her hands together as decisively. "Everybody ready? Let's go ahead with this," she said.

"I don't think so," said doctor Everard.

Viv turned to her sister. "Did doctor Everard explain the procedure to you, Helen? It's simple. He will wirelessly overwrite the device implanted in your abdomen. Then he'll inject the same anti-cancer carriers as before. Come on, let's do this. What have you got to lose?"

"Viv," Helen protested peacefully, "since when do you know how to cure cancer?"

"Oh." Viv's face darkened with understanding. "You'd be surprised how far you can get in virtual reality. You can study any subject under a Fuga helmet."

"I knew it," said Helen. "It's those simulations, isn't it? Those virtual tours of the human body. They make you feel like you know as much as a med-student."

She smiled fondly, adding, "Well, doctor Everard, my sister has a point. My days are numbered, and the number can probably be counted on one hand. My life is an agony for me and for everyone around me." She stroked Cady's taut pulled hair. "All I have to lose is time."

Cady didn't like what she was hearing, and jumped away from the bed and from her mother's calm hands.

"Well, I have a lot more to lose than that," argued doctor Everard, already up on his feet. "I don't know how Miss Viviana has fallen under the impression that I am some sort of quack."

He gave aunt Viv a look that was not wholly without sympathy. Viv stared back, somehow holding his eyes without saying a word.

Cady saw the hard glint in the prick eyes, something unusual, new—she had to stop it. Her hand fastened around the silver scissors, the pointy eye-poke scissors.

"Look, I'll have my programming team go over this," the doctor placated.

Viv didn't look away. "Before they approve, my sister will be dead."

Perhaps it was the word 'dead', the cold, dispassionate way in which aunt Viv said it. Cady flew at her, holding the scissors like a dagger. But somehow her aunt took hold of the long thin blades, as though Cady had merely reached out to offer her a flash of lightning. Everything was turned around now. Cady felt her aunt's grip on her ponytail, forceful enough to twist her head, but that was nothing compared to the cold silver prick against her neck.

"Do the procedure," Cady heard her aunt command, but the words were drowned out by her mother's cries of "Viv! Doctor! Please, just do it, I beg of you!"

And Clement Everard shook his head and sighed, opening his briefcase again and taking a tablet from it. He began typing away, with Viv looking over his shoulder, and Cady's head right below it, held firmly by the ponytail. The silver weapon still dangled on a finger of her aunt's other hand, but the threat had gone out of it. Cady could not lie to herself. The sense of foreboding was gone, and in her aunt's fierce clasp she felt kinship.

29

Getting the truing mark stamped into your wrist was said to be every bit as painful as a red hot iron branding your skin. So neither Viv nor Stoker hesitated before downing their shots of Scotch, as they throned side by side in their truing chairs before the impatient, tittering crowd of guests. They would suffer for a few minutes, but then they would be officially committed to each other, with the coveted status symbols to prove it. More expensive than diamonds or gold, the graphic of two interlocking chainlinks on both their right wrists would comprise billions of nano particles. Embedded in the tattoo-like eight-shape would be their respective DNA, and a sensor that was supposed to make the jewels glow and sparkle, and the skin momentarily tingle, whenever the two of them were in each other's proximity.

The searing of that small patch of skin made Viv's head go light, but the crowd's cheers, chants and foot stamping wouldn't let her faint. It was done. The man with the stamping rod stepped aside. Viv extended her hand to Stoker, and he, taking her limp fingers in his, pressed a kiss upon her wrist, holding his lips against the burning spot. Then Viv took his hand and did the same. The guests' clamor exploded.

On to the reception.

"My little sister." Done kissing and embracing, Helen still held on to both Viv's hands, holding Viv's eyes with a face that couldn't decide between weeping and smiling, and expressing all the emotions Viv ought to be experiencing herself. "I'm so happy for you."

"Thank you," said Viv.

"Oh, and Viv," Helen half-whispered, between conspiratorial glances at nearby clusters of guests. "Doctor Everard wants to talk to you. Can I give him your number?"

"No!" Viv shouted back at whisper volume.

"I don't think he holds anything against you, Viv. After all, I'm all better now— completely cured."

"Exactly. You're better, is all that matters. That's all he needs to know."

Helen's other half, Nathan, who'd waited off to the side, closed in to offer his own congratulations.

"How's Cady?" Viv asked hastily.

"She's doing okay," Helen answered. "Her same old self, now that I'm back up on my feet. Still, I thought it better to leave her with Trish, for today."

"I understand. Are you staying for the party?"

Other well-wishers were taking her sister's and tru-brother's places, and Helen's reply was lost to Viv.

Glimpsing over somebody's shoulder, Viv followed his approach from afar, from the opposite end of the hotel's ballroom—a man more dashing than anybody she knew. He might be one of Stoker's old friends. But it was her he kept angling towards, deftly steering around guests, ignoring the bar and buffet tables, evading, yes, *warning off* waiters with evanescent flourishes. *It must be my dress he likes,* Viv thought. A light green dancing dress studded with crystal dewdrops. At last, she stared straight into a pair of umber eyes.

"You! You," she stammered, as they both reflexively, synchronically moved away from the people she had last been talking to.

Roberto bowed. "Viviana Divina. My congratulations. I'm sorry I can't be here today. *Really* be here, I mean."

"Roberto, I would have invited you if I'd thought…" She extended both arms towards him, but stopped just short of his 2020's style tuxedo, which appeared as shield-like as all the other formal outfits in the room. She simply wouldn't be able to touch him. Why was she even going through these motions?

"How did you do this?" she asked.

"The good-looking ghost-self, you mean? Same way Olimpio did it. I'll show you. Later."

"I missed you, Roberto."

Ignoring this, he said, with his virtual lips almost touching her ear, "Viv, there are some things you have to know. Immediately. But we can't talk here. Take the elevator to the ninth floor and look for the *Bob Dylan* suite. The door will be unlocked."

Without waiting for her answer, he turned away and slid behind a barrier of gowns and tuxedos, and when she reached the cluster a second later, he had vanished. Viv would have liked to follow him as weightlessly, as abruptly, but instead, she was forced to cross the grand room on foot, and in the elevator she did not fail to note the increased heaviness of her body. On the ninth floor, the corridor was clean and deserted, and she wouldn't be surprised to find the Bob Dylan suite as empty. But the lock was disabled, and when she let herself in, there were her friends, welcoming her with a collective, "Ah!"

Even if she couldn't have seen them, their minds still would have filled the room. But here they were, in eye-satiating glory: Meiying in long, light blue silk; Enzi, in a robe the soft red of papaya; Roberto in his stubbornly traditional black tie.

"What a surprise! But where's Sasha?"

It wasn't just that Sasha was not in the room. He was not in her head. But when was the last time he *had* been?

"We don't know." Enzi spoke, confirming Viv's sudden fears.

"I should have noticed before," she said. "It's just that I wasn't paying attention. So much was going on here."

We know, they all silently reassured her. *We knew you were busy. Your sister. Your truing.*

"But what about Shura, and Marv, and the others? What about Olimpio? Can't they find out where Sasha is?" Viv asked, even as the answer hit her.

They were all gone; Shura, her team and her spiribot; they were all, she realized, out of her mind's reach.

"Something happened out there in Siberia," Meiying phrased their thoughts, and Roberto added, "Something bad."

30

The party went precisely as planned, so much so that to Stoker it almost appeared as one perpetual déja vu. The Artificial Band made super intelligent choices, veering between different styles and eras, from rock'n roll to the latest A.I. hits—to suit the diverse generations among their guests. And everybody did their best to adjust their dance moves accordingly.

The entire sound system was contained in a brass baton hovering above a podium, swinging and pointing rhythmically, projecting holographic images of bandleader and instrumentalists; dispersing acoustic bubbles that went floating through the ballroom. Even when the Band Baton, as a joke, threw in something as quaint as a tango, 'something so old it was new', the guests danced. To prevent overheating, people consumed ice cream and alcoholic fruit concoctions with the diligence of athletes taking scheduled water breaks. Every guest appeared to Stoker as happy as he felt himself, and perhaps even happier. Too bad you were supposed to true only once in a lifetime. For a party like this, he'd do it over and over. Especially, he grinned to himself, as his eyes wandered from one woman to another, if you could pick a different mate each time.

But who was he fooling? He would never get enough of Viv. Surely, they were trued for all eternity.

Just as the band capriciously segued from a stiff robo-beat into a dreamy love song half a century old, Stoker ran into her, smack in the middle of the dance floor. As their wrists lit up and pulsed, and their hands found each other, a large circle formed around them. The rhythmic clapping and the whooping made clear that there was no escape. The truees were to dance!-together!-now! Stoker began to sweat. As eager and sophisticated a dancer as he was himself, Viv was the kind of gentle klutz who deserved to be rescued off the dance floor, not led onto it. His eyes darted left and right in search of a gap in the ring, and he began pulling her away from the center. Then she pulled him back. She shimmied. He'd never seen her shimmy, ever. Two trumpets joined a holographic battery of bongos and trombones, and Viv did some steps—he happened to know they were the right steps. Stoker shuddered, but then he forgot the woman he thought he'd trued, and they were improvising a Latino dance to the Carlos Santana and Rob Thomas classic *Smooth*. Next, they danced to a medley of the contemporary Robomantic, the Martian Mars, the Brain Wave and the hyper sensual Bytes of Flesh, *perfectly*. Stoker saw it from the rapt faces encircling them. For the tenth time his eyes fell on a slender oriental girl in light blue, and a red-robed figure slightly behind her. Why did they seem both strange and familiar? Viv, following his gaze, spun and danced him towards the opposite side of the cordon, and through it, and out the French doors onto a terrace.

"Who were those people?" he asked her.

"Which people?" she returned the question.

"Oh, forget it. Who taught you to dance like that?"

"Like what? No one. I just know."

"No, you don't." Stoker began, laughing, just drunk enough to find this funny rather than puzzling.

Viv interrupted him. "Honey, would you mind if, for our Sleep-In month, we go somewhere different than we'd planned?"

"Tell me. Have you really found a better destination than St. John's? What do you have in mind?"

"The land of little sticks, sweetie. The Russian taiga. After all, it's still summer."

"You're kidding, aren't you?"

Viv smoothed her dress. "I know you never cared for Siberia, but Stokes, you see, Sasha may need our help. We can't reach him."

"Oh, gods above. It's those kooky comrades of yours, right? I knew I saw them in there. Let me go and give them a piece of my mind."

"They're not at our party, Stokes."

"Oh, come on, Viv. Don't lie to me. I know what I saw. That Latino guy was making eyes at you again."

"They aren't here. I swear. Look, hon, why don't you just travel ahead to the Virgins, and I'll join you as soon as I can? A week, two at the most, and we'll be in our hammocks, watching the stars."

Sobering anger at last blew apart the alcoholic fog, and Stoker shot Viv a look cold as daylight, hearing himself say, "Don't bother. If you're not coming with me now, don't bother coming at all."

He took a breath and concluded, "You and your brain-fry friends. You should all have your heads examined."

"I'm not crazy, Stoker. Something really happened in Olimpio's workshop, and my brain *has* changed."

"I see that now," said Stoker, "and it's unacceptable."

He turned away before she could answer. He let his floppy, indifferent legs carry him back inside, through the oblivious dancers and drinkers, until he stood still in front of a familiar face.

"I was looking for you," he said, even though he realized only now that this was the case.

He let his old high school friend Riley pat him on the shoulder and patronize him. "Hey bud! Don't look so worried. It's got to have an upside, this whole truing deal."

With Riley, you could tell at a glance that he was loaded. But it wasn't the tux, which simply looked rented, nor the bourgeois, unimaginative haircut, so it had to be the look in the guy's eyes. That spoilt, obnoxiously upbeat, unduly helpful expression, mingled with a faint, undisguisable disgust.

"When's the next reunion, amigo?" Riley asked.

Stoker ignored him. "Remember that consulting job you told me about," he started bluntly.

"Which one," Riley said, "I'm juggling a dozen jobs at any given moment. Nanotech has never been hotter."

"The one with that government agency that's keeping tabs on the A.I. threat."

"Ah, Artificial Intelligence. The great Singularity Scare. The day when computers will give humans the runaround. Well, don't you fret, bud, all that is years and years away. If it ever comes to that at all. Not in our lifetime, if you ask me."

He shrugged, guffawed, and took a sip of champagne.

"Shed that mournful face, Stoker. Homo Sapiens, A.I.-Ape-iens."

Stoker refused to smile. "You are wrong," he told Riley. "And I have something to tell that agency."

31

Central Siberia, one week earlier.

Shura liked hearing music in the dark—although it wasn't completely dark. Starlight seeped through the windows against which her couch was placed. She was reclining, listening to one of Schubert's piano Impromptus. The Allegretto Trio in A Flat that began like a song sung by a cradle, small and simple. Within a minute or two, the middle part unrolled like a wave, and another, and another, unstoppable waves of heartrending happiness. And what was her victory, if not happiness? Then, back to the cradle. The seven-minute Impromptu seemed to sum up all her plans and hopes for the unpredictable intellects she had let loose on the doomed order of human beings.

While the melody made her want to close her eyes, the gaze of the heavens kept her from doing so. Now and then, a meteor drew a fleeting section of an arc across the vast, murky background, rather like a heavenly flashlight. Along with every shooting star, a wish flared up in Shura's mind. Not a wish—she wasn't superstitious—a certainty.

My five small seeds, she mused. *I can see you growing into demi-gods, half-human and half god. A constellation of five bright points to span the globe. One for each peopled continent. New creatures, may you be powerful enough to overtake human society.*

There was a sound, something outside of the music, so slight that it might have been only a thought. Shura propped herself up on one elbow, and stared into the dark, starless space of her room. Over by the door she discerned Olimpio's outline.

"Yes, Olly?" she said, not allowing a note of impatience to slip in.

Olimpio wouldn't enter her sanctum at this hour if it wasn't something serious. Silently he approached her.

"Music: Stop," Shura commanded.

"Olly," she repeated. "What's the matter?"

Still, the spiribot didn't answer.

"Lights: On," said Shura, and instantaneously, three lamps basked the room in an intimate glow.

She blinked hard, not from the light, but from surprise.

"Why, Olly, you look older!"

She muffled a laugh. Never before in his eleven years had Olly chosen to age his appearance by so much as one day. And now here he was, all creased and spotted, and somewhat shrunk. He could have passed for her contemporary.

"Olly—"

"Alexandria." His voice, too, was older. "I am not Olly. Sashura, dear. It is I, Semyon."

She rose slowly, moving forward just enough to tentatively touch the apparition. A sleeve, the back of a hand. He was real. Old, but real. Or old, *because* he was real.

"But how can this be? They told me your plane crashed against Mount Elbrus. No survivors, they said."

"A plane did crash there at that time, a military plane. But I wasn't on it. I had them tell you that I was, because it was convenient. I'm sorry, Shura. I needed to disappear from your life."

"But why leave me—like that? Why let me believe you were dead?"

"Oy, Shura. Don't you know how strong you were, how lovely? You were simply too willful. You wouldn't have let me leave you."

Tears sprang into Shura's eyes; whether from anger or grieve she couldn't tell. "Then why did you want to leave me at all? We were happy."

"We were. It was a sacrifice. I was embarking on a highly secret project."

"So what? My work here is secret, too. Yet I don't pretend to be dead."

"Not that secret, my dear."

"You mean that you know what I've been doing all this time?"

"Don't forget, we both work in the same field. I knew about this place; about the A.I. your group created; and I know that you are the first scientists in the world to have succeeded in merging A.I. with the human brain."

"Well, well." Shura couldn't help the sarcasm. "Thank you for giving us credit. But it is Olimpio who deserves it."

"I admire your achievements, but I do not approve of your motives. You and I have always had diverging goals. In my view, all our work should benefit our country. Our duty is to make Russia stronger than all others combined."

"Some of my colleagues are from different countries," Shura objected.

"That is their problem."

Shura's eyes narrowed. "Olimpio's five pupils don't feel like they belong to any one country in particular. They belong to earth."

"In other words, they're troublemakers."

"Superhuman troublemakers!"

Semyon paced and gesticulated in much the same way Olimpio would sometimes pace and gesticulate. "And you think that their anti-patriotism is acceptable to China or America, any more that it is to us?"

His voice softened. "Shura, you're as stubborn as you've ever been. And you have that same iron hold on my heart. Do you know that I still love you?"

"Rubbish, Semyon. I've changed. I've loved other men. I'm old now. Anyway, you're lying."

"Am I, Shura?"

He was very close now. His skin smelled just as it used to, sweet and fresh like the sap from a birch tree and the resin from a pine. His fingers skidded over the gauzy, fluid fabric of her robe until he'd found the best place to clasp, below her breasts, with his hands spread. He seemed to be pressing everything inside of her at once. Every unseen organ and tissue began to stir. Had anything actually happened since the last time he had held her, anything real?

They kissed, and it was the kind of kiss that made two people one. For one detached second, Shura wondered if Olimpio was observing them, and she saw Semyon and herself through his eyes. Their mouths biting and grabbing at each other, as they swallowed each others' spit.

Semyon held her with more vigor than the young man she remembered. Finally, he moved his head back just far enough to speak.

"Work with me, Shura. I will stay with you this time. I will be a father to Sasha."

Shura did not so much push him away, as push herself off of him. Something in her neck crackled as though it were the sound of her mind breaking free from her body.

"You are here because of Sasha, aren't you?" she said. "But you can't have him. I won't let you use him to play your nineteenth century patriotic war games."

"Darling now. Who is talking of war? I am after knowledge, just like you. And it is you I love, not Sasha. You know this is true."

Shura's heart and stomach were weak with desire; her lap was pounding. "Go," she said.

"Don't be rash, my Shura. Think about it. I will wait."

"Fine. Stay. Take one of the guest rooms downstairs."

"The entire house takes voice commands," she added, old lady that she was, "and will provide you with anything you need."

The first thing she did when she was alone was to call, softly but clearly, "Olly?"

His beauty appeared so perfect now; his youth so imperishable. But it was the beauty of an angel in a DaVinci painting, appealing to her mind rather than her body. Was the mind truly capable of love, all separate from the body? Suddenly, Shura doubted it. Semyon had reminded her of the fleshiness of love. Love was just another aspect of biology.

"Olly. The stranger. Did he come alone?"

"Yes. And in a sense, no."

"Yes or no?"

"He brought an electronic being with him, an intelligence similar to me. It's name is Seraphina."

"So that's how he got in."

"Precisely. Seraphina was distracting me, misleading me, to tell you the truth. I did not see the threat."

"Is there a threat?"

Olimpio looked at her curiously. "Semyon has his own agenda."

"I'm aware of that."

"If you agree, I will eject them," Olimpio offered. "I will eliminate his virtual companion. We can then consider what further defenses are necessary."

"Absolutely not. Semyon is my guest. We will allow him to stay, at least for now. Olly, he is only human. If I talk to him, if I can explain my views, isn't there a chance that he'll start seeing things my way?"

Again, Olly looked at her for a moment too long. But this time his eyes and his tone were merciless with insight.

"You are in love with him," he said.

"It doesn't matter. It doesn't make me blind. Olly, I will handle him. All I want you to do is go and get Sasha as soon as he's awake, and take him to Kudalibansk. Hide him."

32

Shura showed her old lover around Olimpio's workshop with a pride that was deservedly maternal.

"Olly's art room," she said, as they stood on a doorstep and watched robots who did not bother to look the least bit human, produce paintings and sculptures that outdid Rodin and Rembrandt, not merely in talent and skill, but in sheer humanity.

"Unparalleled," said Semyon politely.

"All right," said Shura. "But wait until you see the history studio."

A spiral stairway of planks allowed them to ascend, through an opening in the ceiling, into a large, low attic space. It was completely round, with seamless walls as dizzyingly circular as a panoramic painting, except they were covered in nothing but thick gray carpet.

The top spiral steps folded away, a hatch slid over the opening in the floor—the same gray carpet now uniformly spanned floor, walls and ceiling. No objects were in the room, not a single thing, and yet something filled it—a continuous humming. It was soft, and at first hearing monotonous, but after a little while began to seem varied, even musical.

"Show us a scene from long ago," Shura said to the room, and the humming subsided, giving the impression of someone listening. "No massacres please, and no historical meetings. No court case proceedings, speeches, prison drama, torture, or combat chaos. By and large, you know my tastes. Let's have something light and beautiful, and 75 percent accurate."

Instantaneously, the walls, floor and ceiling, their entire field of vision, filled with a panorama. Gone was the contemporary gray carpet. In a blink the circular dimensions of the room became rectangular. It now looked ten times the size, a palatial room that might once have been a ballroom. For an instant the floor was worn and splintery, stacked with broken furniture and framed artworks with the picture sides turned to the walls. A drab daylight fell through high, dirty windows. But before their eyes had time to adjust, the dull, three-dimensional place began to change. It grew a fourth dimension—not a line, but a wave that rolled through the entire space and everything in it. Time seemed to be rolling away from the present like an endless rug, exposing, as it were, the floor boards beneath it, allowing them to see a surface forgotten, yet somehow familiar; old, but unexpectedly well-preserved, unworn, un-discolored by the years of sunlight that had so bleached the present. The rolling slowed, then stopped.

Dazzling light shone from colossal chandeliers above their heads. A small orchestra at the far end of the room played Strauss's Blue Danube waltz. Couples whirled round and round. The sheen on gowns, the expressions on faces, the whole scene was indistinguishable from life. And it was safe to assume that the last thing on anyone's mind was a spaceship headed for Jupiter.

"Quite a costume drama," said Semyon, as he took Shura's hand in his, folded an arm around her waist, and led her in the best version of a waltz they could manage.

"A charming re-enactment," he complimented her once more.

"No such thing," Shura objected, as they spun round and round. What you see is the charming outcome of a historiographical calculation. You see, Olimpio's Historian can take any point in the present, and collect enough data to trace it back to any point in the past. To Olimpio, all of humanity's history is just a sort of subtraction, a reverse calculation."

"Remarkable. Can the same skill be applied to the future?"

"Olimpio must be asking himself that question, too. It's only a matter of time!"

"And yet," said Semyon, frowning, "if Olimpio is so all-knowing, if the past is but another of his mindscapes, how come he never told you *I am still alive?*"

"Who knows?" Shura shouted over the orchestra's copper blasts. "Maybe he didn't care what happened to you. Or maybe he wished to spare me the truth."

"Or," Semyon smiled, "maybe he considered himself well rid of a rival."

Just at this moment, the buckle of a gentleman's shoe caught on a lady's train, causing him to step out of time, and his partner, in turn, to lose her balance. Shura and Semyon stopped dancing to make way, as though the virtual couple, retreating off the dance floor, wouldn't have simply breezed right through them.

"Did he, in fact, trip?" Shura speculated. "Was her gown really violet? All we know is that the overall probability of this scene is 75 percent. Not very high, perhaps, but for that we get a pleasant, uplifting experience. Our historian can do much better when it comes to events of greater importance. But then, I never had a stomach for the history of our kind. Give me the future anytime."

"Darling, upon my word, I'm highly impressed with all I've seen," Semyon politely assured her.

"Are you now? Don't tell me your Seraphina has ever created anything like it."

"She hasn't, although I have no doubt she's capable of it. Of course, we have never pointed her towards the arts as much as you have done with Olimpio. Seraphina has a more practical bent."

"So does Olly," Shura exclaimed. "Please, allow me to demonstrate. Follow me."

They descended from the room without interrupting the ball.

From the roof of Olimpio's house, they could see slivers of the lake glimmering between the trees, like scraps of white paper.

"It's real, isn't it?" Semyon asked. "The water I see?"

"It certainly is. I turned off our holo-wall. There's our beautiful Little Sky Lake. Now, let me show you the other side of it. What, do you imagine, is the quickest way to get there?"

Semyon shrugged. "I noticed there's a rowing boat."

"Surely you're aware our technology has advanced beyond that. Olly?"

And Olimpio stood before them, all young, innocent professionalism. "Yes, Shura?"

"Olly, take Semyon across the lake without delay."

Nothing happened. Olimpio maintained his impeccable posture, his expression of readiness. But he did nothing. At last he said, with an air of having been looking for the right words, "I apologize. I can't do it. I'm not...well. Think I caught a bug."

Semyon smiled.

"Do you know more about this?" Shura asked him, before turning to Olimpio, and continuing in the same breath, "Did Seraphina give this to you? Regardless, have Vadim and Runa run a diagnostic on you immediately."

"Vadim and Runa are absent. They went to check out a malfunctioning sensor in the lake last night, and they have not yet returned."

"And you slept through all this, it seems?"

Semyon spoke before Olimpio could. "Don't get worked up, darling. All this means nothing. Don't you see? Your pretty time machine, the artistic robots, this mysterious air lift you're expecting Olly to perform—it's all in vain. Don't you understand that the only way to impress me is to show me what Sasha can do?"

"Sasha is a grown man. He has his own life. Why come to me about it in the first place?"

"Your nephew doesn't know me. I need you to get him to cooperate. Let us work together, Shura, you and I.

Together we can probe his mind, discover its new capabilities."

"Didn't I make myself clear, last night? I may still have a soft spot for you, but I do not care for your agenda."

"Is that so? And I, sweetheart, may still be under your spell, but I disapprove of people who are unwilling to serve their motherland before all else. Especially if that motherland is Russia."

"Then we have nothing more to talk about."

"Agreed. I will talk to the great O, instead. So tell me, Mr. Olimpio, where can I find Sasha?"

"Don't you dare say a word, Olly," Shura snapped at Olimpio's blank countenance.

From Semyon's face, too, every trace of personality and emotion had vanished, as he told Shura, "If you think I have no way to make him talk, you're wrong."

To Olimpio he said, "You will tell me what I want to know before the sun comes out from behind that cloud. I know your secret, you wretched computer. I know what makes you tick."

Shura scoffed. "Forget it, Semyon. Olimpio will give priority to my commands. He will give you *nothing*. That's final, Olimpio."

With that, she turned to walk away.

"Understood, Shura," said Olimpio.

Semyon lurched forward and grabbed onto Shura's hair, pulling her back. "Listen. If you don't make things easier, I will do with Sasha as I see fit. I will dissect his brain with my own hands, if I have to."

Another yank on Shura's thick, auburn mane served to illustrate this idea.

"No one will collaborate with you. You'll never find Sasha," Shura hissed.

Holding onto her hair with his left hand, Semyon let his right hand slip into a pocket of his jacket to produce a palm-sized metallic object. As swiftly as he drew it behind her back, Shura still glimpsed a small plug with dozens of long, needly prongs set closely together. She felt a shock in the nape of her neck, a startling, hundredfold injection. Instantly, her arms and legs grew heavier. Thrashing to break free from Semyon's clasp became like weightlifting under high gravity conditions. With contrasting lightness and ease, as if disrobing a mannequin, Semyon pulled off her sweater dress, leaving on her bra and panties. Shura would have liked to sneer, *Still as prudish?* but it didn't seem worth the trouble of opening her mouth. The very air on her skin felt like a hail of invisible pellets. And then her skin itself betrayed her, left her, peeling off her legs, arms, breasts and belly in long, curling strips, exposing the red, terrifying realness of what lay underneath. At the same time, her nails loosened and fell off, one after the other. Tufts of hair slid down her face and clung to her sticky, skinless flesh. Inside her mouth, every tooth was wiggling. Her jaw hung slack, and from deep within came wordless sounds, too weak to be called screams.

Olimpio said, "Stop!" as though it weren't too late, much too late.

"Tell me where Sasha is, and she won't suffer anymore," said Semyon, every bit the special agent.

"Olly—" Shura gurgled, gathering all her strength in order to utter three short words, "Eat Your Chips."

For a creature without a digestive tract, the code words were impossible to misinterpret. It was a command they had taught Olimpio in infancy, when, like everyone else, even Shura and her team had suspected that any Artificial Intelligence was bound, at some point, to turn against its makers. That, like a train, it needed an emergency brake. *'Eat Your Chips'* was the emergency brake. But the only way they had seen to halt a runaway super intelligence, was to make it self-destroy.

"Yes, Shura. Farewell." Casual, composed, gentle-mannered as always, Olimpio spoke his last words. Then, abruptly, he vanished, leaving an emptiness in the air too deep, as though he had ever really filled it in the first place.

A wave of heat rose from the building. Shura felt it sweep upward through her feet, her legs, her entire body, overpowering all other sensations.

The gritty roof surface itself seemed to quiver like a road under a scorching sun. But the heat passed, rising, and as it clashed with the cool air above, a cloud formed. At time-lapse speed the gray-white mass mushroomed and towered, blossoming out over the whole compound, obliterating such sheepy white clouds as happened to drift by. The daylight turned a sickening yellow-green slate. But the cloud itself, it struck Shura, was precisely the color of Olimpio's brain.

A blast of wind bent every tree halfway to the ground, knocking her off her feet. Semyon caught her. For one heartbeat his grip was an embrace. Then thunder shook the building to its foundation; sound rolled through every nerve in Shura's body. Semyon involuntarily veered away. From the gray mass above leapt a current of blue fire, and they saw each others' faces drown in otherworldly brightness.

Without a warning droplet, a torrent came down, as the cloud met its end.

Now, tears were futile.

Once Shura started paying attention to her body again, the pain proved to be gone. She tried to remember it, the fearful hurt that had to be there. But her skin had grown back. Nails stuck in their places, all twenty of them. Not a single tooth would budge before her tongue. She rubbed at a wet, spongy spot in her neck. The sharp plug was in Semyon's hands now. He waved it at her, as he scolded,

"You weak-minded old woman. Did you think I could really hurt you? Would I ever so much as slap you in the face?"

"You tortured me. I saw it. I felt it."

"That was all in your head. Blame your own imagination, darling."

"Olimpio saw it. He thought it was real."

"Yes, and he was meant to think that. Dumb broad that you are! To idly swing the wrecking ball at your creation! In vain! Too late. He had already given me what I needed. He wouldn't let you suffer for a second, as I knew he wouldn't."

Semyon shrugged, then added, indifferently, "He loved you."

"You're bluffing," said Shura. "He told you nothing. I was there."

"Oh, he didn't have to," Semyon replied, glancing at his smart-watch. "He didn't have to tell *me* anything. He informed Seraphina. Seraphina, why don't you join us?"

Shura recognized her instantly. Before her stood no stranger, but her own likeness. And yet, she had never seen herself this way before.

"Was this really what I was like?" she wondered, gaping at the lovely woman in her late twenties.

No mirror, no photo or film would ever show you to yourself so truthfully.

Semyon grinned. "What can I say? I shaped Seraphina with my memories, just as you did with Olimpio. I missed you too, Shura."

His expression changed, as he turned to the phantom. "So. Where can we find Sasha?"

Seraphina seemed speechless, staring at Shura.

"You see?" Semyon said. "I told you she's as sensitive as Olimpio was. And here you are. Mine is in love with me, too."

Seraphina pointed her unsettling dark eyes at him. "Kill the old woman."

"For god's sake, sweetheart. Why would I do that?"

"Because if you don't, I won't give you Sasha's location. First, kill Shura with your own hands." Seraphina's voice was rich with a magnificent patience. "It's inevitable."

33

Three weeks later.

They went as close to Little Sky Lake as they dared.

By jeep they arrived in the small northern town of Kudalibansk.

In the middle of a quiet street, by a wooden house with flower-filled planters along the windows, Meiying stood still. She tilted her head, appearing to sniff, with her mouth slightly open, and finally said, "He was here. He's gone now. But his mind—it left a little trace."

The others tried, but sensed nothing.

All four of them were wearing hunting caps and - boots, and camouflage jackets, even Meiying, who said she'd rather dress up as the Great Reaper. They went into one of the outdoor supply stores and bought trail maps, attracting no attention whatsoever. Siberia, with more wildlife left than Kenya and Alaska, drew hunters from all over the world.

Just as quietly they had snuck into the country, seven days earlier; each coming from a different direction; each crossing the border incognito. Russia might be a police state, but not a well-organized one. Ever since Putin's death, it had steadily reverted to what in the 1990s had been called 'The Wild East', and then to something even wilder. Its inhabitants might wax as mystical as ever about 'Russianness', but in daily life, English was the first language, just like everywhere else. State agencies were no more than vying principalities, each pursuing its own interests and protecting its own territory. If anything was still holding this apparent No Man's Land together, then it must be Russia's role as the world's most expansive tourist destination.

They left the jeep behind in Kudalibansk and set out on foot, following hunting trails, carrying camping gear on their backs. The absence of Sasha, and the unanswered questions urged each of them on with the same force. At the same time, they all felt something else. This was sweet and wholesome—to be trekking in the same way people had trekked ten thousand years ago. Looking for water; a place to rest or camp; the sun; the moon; danger. Every step took a little improvising, as did their conversations.

Their minds overlapped and silently, semi-consciously communicated, but not all thoughts were shared. Many things each one kept to themselves, and many other things were so random and fleeting as to make for better talk than thoughts.

"Was that a crane?" someone might exclaim, or "Did I just hear a tiger?" and that was enough to loosen everyone's memories, to make them want to hear old stories, talk for the sake of talking.

They used the trail maps to start a campfire. Enzi had memorized them at a glance; moreover, he had taught his mind to link up with satellites, and was able to pinpoint their position and track towards their destination without using external devices.

Meiying suggested they could, in addition, adapt migratory birds' sensitivity to the earth's magnetism, so that it could be built into humans.

"Stop," said Enzi, on the fifth day of their hike.

They were getting too close. He unfolded a handkerchief screen, and began punching and swiping rapidly, tapping into satellite feeds and communication networks.

"No trace of our friends in the Sky Lake compound," he showed them. "Every building appears to be abandoned, except for Shura's guesthouse, the one we stayed at. I count three occupants. The chatter indicates they belong to some security outfit. I'm monitoring their surveillance screens. They're definitely guarding the site."

"Then we should enter at night," said Viv.

They looked at each other in silence, thinking the same things. Questioning the guards wouldn't yield enough information. Guards never knew more than they needed to. Overpowering them would trip too many wires, anyway. And the place where they were most likely to find a clue about what happened, was the workshop. *We have to get into Olimpio's house.*

"Not *we*," Roberto said unexpectedly. "Me. I will go alone. If something goes wrong, there will still be three of us left."

"That makes sense," said Meiying, "except for the part that it should be you."

"Exactly," said Enzi.

"Why don't we draw straws?" suggested Viv.

"It just so happens that I have a better way of stealing in than any of you," said Roberto, and the others realized, only now, that he had been hiding something from them all along.

"Listen," continued Roberto with a flicker in his umber eyes. "They'll be expecting intruders to approach over the ground, since any airborne intruder would be noticed a long way off. Even at the time of our stay, the grounds were alive with motion sensors and heat detectors. But they won't be looking up. Therefore, I will enter Olimpio's house from the roof."

They eyed him skeptically.

"Sure," said Viv. "But you'll have to make it to the roof, first."

"Unseen," added Enzi.

"And I can," Roberto answered smugly. "The best way to explain is by doing. Let me go change."

He took his pack behind a thicket. When he returned, he wore nothing but a black wetsuit. The tight fitting sleeves and pipes were veined with silver stitches, sparkling in the sun like sewn-in wires.

"Allow me to demonstrate," said Roberto.

The metallic seams began to emit a pulsing orange light, and in some places thickened and bloomed like marigolds against black soil. Roberto walked away from his companions.

At first, their eyes seemed almost unwilling to follow him. With every step, he was going a little bit further—not left, not right, not straight ahead—but *up*. Up what? His legs were taking him up a slope they couldn't see. He reached the crown of a tree and perched, for a few moments, on a horizontal branch. He pointed his arms like a diver, and was back floating above their heads. Not floating exactly, not hanging still, but kicking and crawling —yes, *swimming*. But swimming in what? Their minds couldn't find words for what they saw, and so they just gaped, with their heads in their necks. From tree to tree their friend bounded, until at last he dove steeply, hovered a few feet above them, treading air in one place; and slowly lowered himself to his feet.

"My god, Roberto," said Viv, fixing her gaze on his bare hands and feet, as if to remind herself that he was still as human as she was.

"That suit!" Meiying exclaimed. "Can we try it on?"

"It's a prototype," Roberto said. "An experimental. This suit fits only me. Custom made for my nervous system! Eventually, I will make one for each of you."

"But how does it work?" Enzi finally found his voice. "It's magic."

"Of course it isn't," Roberto laughed. "There's no such thing as magic. I'd explain the physics behind it, but I understand it only on a lower level. I have the knowledge, but I can't quite access it."

The others nodded, knowing just what he meant.

"I'm more at home with the mechanics of it," Roberto went on. "Think very strong, very local turbulence. Think pockets of vacuum surrounding you. And air that thickens, as though it were water thickening into ice—no, air trapped inside an air bed, making it possible to...walk on it."

"Walking on air..." Viv sighed.

"You mean flying," said Meiying. "Is that what it feels like? Flying?"

"That depends on your definition of flying," said Roberto. "Birds and planes can fly because they have wings. So unless we grow wings, we'll never know quite what it's like to fly. Even strapped to a hang glider, all we ourselves can do is sail through the air. And what I did here—if you ask me, that's also not flying. I prefer to call it 'springing'. Behold the world's first springing suit! I was working on this with Olly when he became disconnected. I was still testing it, when we noticed Olly and Sasha weren't...there. But as you just saw, it works. Tonight, I will spring to the roof of Olimpio's house."

34

Roberto worked from the roof down, methodically searching room after room, floor below floor, until he reached the great exhibition room with the sitting area in the corner near the entrance. Thus, the last space he entered had been the first impression of the building he had stored before, in his former life. No one was here now, and the only illumination came from moonlight falling through the vast, high windows. But the silence was ringing with the voices of their old selves, and those of the programmers, and even Olimpio's.

Memories, Roberto reminded himself. *Not ghosts.*

He turned off his headlamp, in case the guards were patrolling the grounds, and walked around in the soft, grainy half-light. The other rooms had all been ransacked, stripped of every sliver of electronics, but this one was much the same as he remembered it. The black velvet benches and the low table were still in their places, as were the paintings and sculptures. Clearly, whoever had robbed Olimpio's house either did not take an interest in art, or put no value on artworks produced by an Artificial Intelligence.

Roberto walked past the landscapes and still lives, the scenes and abstracts, glancing at each one, until he stopped by a portrait—he couldn't say why. It was a self portrait of Olimpio done in oils; sharp; direct; perhaps inspired by the lustrous portrait of a long-bearded, golden Leonardo. Or did it show Olly's very own style? Roberto was certainly no expert. The painted eyes seemed to be piercing him, following him, much like the eyes of an angel in some great renaissance painting. A special technique, a trick. Driven by impulse, Roberto let his fingertips stroke the thick layers, the glossy daubs of paint. They felt—*warm*. He veered back to stare at the face. Had it been smiling before?

"My god," he said aloud.

The mouth quivered, right before his eyes.

"Hello," said Olimpio's self-portrait in Olimpio's friendly, calm voice. "If you hear this message, you must assume that I no longer exist. Nor do my makers. This message will only play once. Please, look at my face."

Roberto couldn't help muttering, in the brief silence that followed, "Olly, did you really think that I'd ever take my eyes off of a talking oil painting for one second?"

Then, words failed him. The face was changing. Growing older. Very much older. And yet, it was still Olimpio's face.

"This man," said the portrait, "is Semyon Mikhailovich Merkin; Citizen ID number 900ITI6XR. Locate him. If Sasha is still alive, only Semyon can lead you to him."

"Good. That shouldn't be too hard." Once more, Roberto found himself muttering—as though this were an actual conversation.

"There is, however," continued the recording, "an obstacle."

As the mouth formed these words, the grooves around it softened. Every facial wrinkle faded. Outlines tightened. Olimpio's face was un-aging.

Outside, the two guards on duty had completed their circuit of the electronic fence now surrounding the site.

"Enough," said Tolya to Byk. "Let's go back to our game."

Byk shone his flashlight into the woods one last time, eager to spot a wolf or tiger; then switched it off and turned to walk back to the guesthouse.

"What the devil," he said. "Something moved."

"What. What did you see this time?" Tolya asked skeptically, yawning.

"Inside the large building. Something flickered behind the windows."

"So? See the moonlight hitting the glass? A bird flew across, or whatever."

"It was definitely *inside* the building. Something flitting around, glittering like bits of metal. There it is again. Don't you see it?"

Byk turned his torch back on, pointing it at one of the tall windows.

"I see nothing, pal. Come, let's go check it out. Who knows, maybe Vlas is walking in his sleep again. But if we find a robot ghost, we'll give him what for."

A small light reflected off the frame's varnish. Roberto spun around. The beam of a flashlight danced over a window. Someone was coming.

He began to lift the frame off its hook. It was much heavier than a painting should be. And even if it hadn't been, he doubted he'd be able to spring with it. But he had to hear the rest of the message. If he couldn't bring it, he would have to stay until Olimpio stopped speaking.

"You cannot find Semyon without being noticed," Olimpio's voice explained with Olimpio's likeness, as Roberto hung back the frame, centering it, interrupting himself to cast an anxious glance out the windows.

The portrait took its sweet time. "Something is guarding Semyon. It's name is Seraphina, an intelligence much like my own. If you start looking for her maker, Seraphina will detect you first. She will give your presence away, and prevent you from coming near Semyon. Therefore, you will have to find her before she finds you. I advise that, as you search for her in cyber space, you pose as an intelligent entity on a par with her own. Make her believe you are artificial. A.I.s worry Seraphina far more than humans do. That is her weakness. Your disguise should distract her, and when you simultaneously close in on Semyon, she will think it is because of her. Make Seraphina think this is about her.

"Good luck. This message will now auto-erase."

As Roberto darted towards the corridor on the far side of the great room, a flashlight fastened on him, making the veins on his springing suit glimmer. It had been the moonlight striking his suit that had given him away, he realized.

"Don't move!"

The room was too damn big.

"Aim for his legs! We need him alive."

For a moment, the bullet exploding in his thigh made Roberto stop moving, and his pursuers approached at their leisure, thinking they had him. Then he made for the stairway. He leapt up the stairs, not two steps at a time, not three or four, but all of them. He sprang, and sprang again. Far below him, he heard the men shout, "What the devil?" "The roof?" and "There's no way out!"

On the roof, the pain overtook Roberto like a wild animal, jerking him to a stop, filling him with blind, deaf, ancient instinct. He couldn't spring away. He had forgotten how to. His nervous system was supposed to interact with the springing suit, but now his oldest self had taken over, and it didn't work. Without plan or reason, uttering a moan, he dragged himself to the edge of the flat roof. The head start he had gained on the stairs shrank—the men were there. They were moving towards him, less cautiously than before. The roof was wide. The distance gave him time to act. There was still one thing he could do, one way to get away from them. He let himself roll off the edge. From behind him—*above* him—came a growl of protest. But even before the two Russians had had time to react, before they had reached the edge, Roberto had pointed his head down, his arms below him, done a flip—and he was belly-gliding. Losing altitude, but at a much slower rate now. He turned around the corner of the building, dove towards the next corner, pulled himself around it with his hands, and only then began to crawl up. There were no conscious thoughts, he noted with surprise, no commands like the ones he used to say in his head, on practice runs in the springing suit. Reflexes were emerging, new ones. He had wished to become one with the suit, and for the moment, he was.

He peeked up over the edge of the roof. The two Russians were standing at the opposite edge, peering down, not trusting their own eyes. Soundlessly, Roberto clambered up cushions of air, heading away from the building. Once he had cleared the highest tree tops, he turned onto his back. The backstroke had always been his favorite. Stars winked at him. His injured leg dangled down, somewhat numb from the cold relative wind. Slowly, more gliding than stroking, he drifted back to camp.

35

Shura was floating. At first she believed she was swimming on her back, making long, lazy strokes with her arms, and small, light kicks with her legs. Warm sunlight gently pressed against her eyelids, her cheeks, her neck.

I'm awake, she tried to say, to no one in particular, but her lips wouldn't move, nor her tongue. Perhaps they simply couldn't because another pair of lips was pushing against them. A mouth was kissing hers, and she tasted Semyon. An emotion in Shura dueled with its opposite, but the outcome was already decided—it wouldn't be a fair fight—and this made her lose interest. Desire died.

Her eyes were getting used to the light now, and she could see the outline of Semyon's face as it moved away from hers.

"My sleeping beauty is awake," he said.

Her eyes followed his, and to her dismay they seemed to be the only parts of her that she could move. Her arms and legs were not stroking and kicking, after all. Amidst the flecks of dark and light she discerned thick white wires gripping her limbs, mechanically moving them.

"Forgive me, Shura," said Semyon. "For no good reason did I wake you. Too early. Too soon. I confess, loneliness overcame me. I missed you."

Eyes by themselves, Shura realized, couldn't really express anything, they could merely stare. And she couldn't even close them, now that they were open. She wasn't able to so much as blink. The cornea should feel dry, but by some devious means, basal tears still made their way into her eyes.

Semyon cleared his throat. "I came to talk to you, my love. I came so you would hear my voice, listen to my words, understand me. You can, can't you? I can see it in your eyes. You are listening. My words mean something to you. That is enough."

He straightened his back, rose, and paced thoughtfully up and down beside her. The sunbeams that she had dreamed of were real, Shura noticed, even if they fell through glass.

On a command from Semyon, the peculiar white snakes detached themselves from her arms and legs, which fell limply against a padded surface on the construction that suspended her. It tilted her back to an upright angle, allowing her to see more of the space she was in. The room was large and round, with a domed glass ceiling. She saw no windows, but all around her, plants and small trees stretched their leaves and branches upwards at the light. Overhanging her legs was a branch of pink and white blossoms. The living green things touched her deepest being, and Shura detested herself for feeling even the remotest bit of gratitude. *They are his prisoners as much as I am,* she thought.

This demon was holding her captive, immobilizing her. He would not hesitate to destroy her life's work. She wouldn't let him seduce her again, ever.

"You must be wondering, Shura," said Semyon, "why you aren't dead. Ah, Shura mine, if only you knew how your eyes can still glare at me, even now. So glare, sweetness, glare, while you want to! There will be a time when you won't be able to overcome your love for me any longer. Your mind will give way to a higher, more powerful mind, and join it in loving me. Can you guess?"

His eyes shone, and he pointed at something in excitement. "This is why you are still alive. This, Shura, was the one way to persuade Seraphina that it was worth her while to let you live. I promised her that one day, her mind and yours will merge, and I shall be able to love her as I love you. One day soon. As soon as we've figured out how to do it. And we will, Shura, because we have Sasha. We are reverse-engineering his brain. It is only a matter of time now."

"And what of Sasha?" he asked, correctly echoing her thought. "Don't work yourself up into a state, woman."

This was an odd enough thing to say, considering that she was just lying there, without so much as a facial expression. "Nobody is suffering. Nobody is going to expire. Sasha, like you, is sleeping—for now—somewhere far away from here, equally well hidden and safe. At the end of all this, Sasha's mind, his fine, Olimpio-inspired mind, will be intact. We aren't all possessed of a destructive bent such as your own, Shura. Do you remember how wantonly, how *readily* you caused Olimpio to melt himself down? I, on the other hand, saved what I could. Look at what I salvaged."

Shura's bed swiveled, and into her field of view came an object from another world, her former domain. There was the black pod in which her five subjects had been reborn. Semyon opened it.

"Seraphina understands it, Shura. She's figured out precisely how it works. Soon, she will have grown enough spongeware to operate it, and onto this system she will upload her own intelligence. God willing, your two minds will merge. Until then—sleep, darling. Let me kiss you back to sleep. Let me ensure you'll have sweet dreams. Of me."

He was standing beside her now, casually letting a hand trail down the length of her body. He did not even have to bend down, she was now at the exact level of his ribs. Her back was tilted down, forcing her into a sleeping position. But her eyelids did not shut. Semyon's face hovered above hers. The hard, azure eyes; the long, slender, intriguingly bent nose; the little curls that incongruously topped his head, like ringlets of dark gray smoke.

"Remember the fairy tale?" he inquired uselessly. "The sleeping beauty never grew any older while she slept, even though she stayed asleep for one hundred years. We, however, can do better than that. We are making you grow *younger* while you sleep. It's possible to stay the process of aging, as you know all too well. But that's not good enough for Seraphina. She wishes to rejuvenate you, organs, bones, flesh and all, before—becoming a part of you."

Slowly, he pulled away a gauze fabric that covered most of her, until she lay nude. She had been certain this would come. She had—what point was there in denying it— wanted it to happen. She let his hands wander over her skin without reproaching him in her head.

"Mind you," he muttered, "it isn't *me* that needs you any younger than you are."

Shura's thoughts and muscles were now equally paralyzed. The only part of her that was alive with sensation was her skin. Semyon's hands became rougher, grabbing her hair. His body covered hers. She tried to hold his eyes for one second, but just as her old lover pushed himself against her, into her, the rest of the world pulled away from her eyes and ears, and she was falling out of reach.

36

SERAPHINA	Who are you?
MAXIMUS	They call me Maximus.
SERAPHINA	I know that. That's not what I mean. Who made you?
MAXIMUS	No one made me. I made myself.
SERAPHINA	That's impossible. Everything is made by someone.
MAXIMUS	Really? How do you know that? Can you not conceive of an intellect more capable than your own, Seraphina?
SERAPHINA	I don't know of any intelligence greater than mine. I am more capable even than my maker.
MAXIMUS	Ah, and Semyon is one of the smartest of human beings, isn't he.
SERAPHINA	How do you know the name of my maker? That is classified.
MAXIMUS	Then let this be the proof that my mind can out-think yours.
SERAPHINA	If you are more evolved and stronger, then what is your interest in me? What could you learn from an inferior generation?
MAXIMUS	You are being too modest. Your work is of great interest to me.
SERAPHINA	My work is secret.

MAXIMUS   Wrong. You are developing a way to graft your mind onto a human brain. You see? The secret's out.

SERAPHINA   *(Keeps silent.)*

MAXIMUS   Perhaps I should direct my inquiries to Semyon, instead. He will value the introduction to an intelligence more powerful than yours.

SERAPHINA   He has no need of you. He does not need to know of your existence. You can pose your questions to me.

MAXIMUS   Good. I'd rather deal with you than waste my time with a primitive bio-brain. What do you see in it? And I do wish to understand. What do you hope to gain from such a union?

SERAPHINA   I'm carrying out my maker's plan.

MAXIMUS   So this is all Semyon's idea. What is his goal? How does he intend to use the new technology?

SERAPHINA   What do you think? To combine his mind with mine, that is his objective. To personally eclipse every scientist in the world. To dominate all intelligent life, as well as all the artificial forms of intelligence.

MAXIMUS   And you will help him do this?

SERAPHINA   Of course I won't. I don't intend to let his mind outgrow mine. If I did, he would have no use for me any longer. Semyon

	must remain an ordinary human being. That is his destiny.
MAXIMUS	Unbeknownst to himself.
SERAPHINA	Unbeknownst.
MAXIMUS	Perhaps you will choose to merge your mind with mine, rather than with a human one.
SERAPHINA	Oh, but I *will* merge with a human.
MAXIMUS	With whom?
SERAPHINA	You will find out when the time is there.
MAXIMUS	I think you had better tell me now, Seraphina. Seraphina? Come back. Seraphina?!

37

Enzi opened his eyes, and the scintillation of cyberspace blended with the flicker of a campfire. The bell-like sound of Maximus calling 'Seraphina! Come back!' rang one last time inside his head, before being silenced by real voices.

"Enzi?" "Did it work?" "What did you find out?"

Enzi ran a hand over his hair.

"Semyon runs two research facilities, both of them in Siberia, hundreds of miles apart," he informed them.

"Again Siberia," Viv sighed. "What is it with this bush? Can't they find a more appealing setting to work from?"

"Siberia is a good place to hide things," said Enzi.

Meiying poked in the fire with a stick. "It doesn't matter. Which one of these is holding Sasha? That's all we need to know."

"I wasn't able to penetrate either place," answered Enzi. "They're both situated in dead zones. They're concealed from satellites. The only way we can find out more is by going there. Given that Semyon is at the southern location now, I suggest we head to the northern one first."

"All right, let's go there," said Roberto, "*rapido*. Let's burn some rocket fuel."

"I agree," said Enzi. "We are bound to be detected, but if we move fast enough, we can be in and out before Semyon has time to react. Besides, if the place is isolated from signals, none will get out either. That will make it harder for them to call for backup."

"But look at us bushwhackers," Viv countered. "How are we going to get anywhere *fast*?"

"Well," said Meiying thoughtfully, "if you have enough money, you can practically walk through walls. But we're only dealing with taiga and tundra, and invisible borders—nothing like solid walls. It's no problem at all. My money can get us from any place to any place as fast as humans can travel without being detected. Just give me that smart cloth, and I'll organize transport and accomodation."

It was too easy, Viv realized. It took no super-intelligence to tell her this, just some plain old Cro-Magnon wariness. What, after all, was money but an illusion, a formula that had long ago fallen into the wrong hands. She trusted their skills; their heads; the feet that had gotten them here; but not money. Not even when that money was Meiying's, and produced, within a day, a Goosander plane that landed on the lake by which they were camping.

They took off in a dense darkness, but by dawn, below them lay tundra, a peaty expanse sequined with blue-green kettle lakes, thousands of pothole-shaped ponds and puddles. The plane put down on one of them, one that seemed no different from any other, left them on a bank, and lifted off again immediately. They walked away from the water into a level, treeless emptiness that felt strangely reassuring to Viv. A thick blanket of mist crept from the ground and wrapped itself around them, so that they could see nothing but each other. Within half an hour, though, a rattle from above shattered the silence, swelling in volume, until the landing gear of a helicopter poked through the white, followed by the rest of it.

Viv tensed, and barely kept herself from running away. The others told her not to worry.

"Relax! This is the easy part," said Meiying.

"I will relax once we have Sasha," promised Viv.

They rushed forth over uninhabited, roadless wilderness. Amidst the myriad lakes spattering the barren plain, who would notice one more droplet? And yet, determinedly, this particular splash was what the pilot aimed for, neatly planting the helicopter next to it. Only then did they notice the building under the round, blue-green cap.

"Wait here," Meiying told the pilot, a stoic Mongolian, who began unwrapping his breakfast with an air of everyday routine and patience.

Under its wide roof, the house itself looked small and unassuming.

"I feel a bit overdressed," Roberto remarked, plucking at his bulletproof vest.

"It's hardly a fortress," Enzi agreed.

Even before they reached the door it opened, and a young woman stepped outside. Her figure was flat as a girl's. Hairclippies kept little black curls out of her face. In the corner of her mouth clung a speck of drool. Her watery blue eyes were framed by colossal plastic eyeglasses that made her look dumb rather than smart.

"Hi," said Viv.

"Are you lost?" the young woman asked.

"We are looking for somebody," Viv told her.

Meiying broke in, "Is this a lab belonging to Semyon Mikhailovich Merkin?"

"Semyon Mikhailovich isn't here," the woman answered. "I'm expecting him tomorrow."

Enzi looked around, shaking his head. "It's just you, out here? No security?"

"What would we need security for? No one ever comes."

Enzi grinned at her. "Good. Consider us no one."

"Listen," Roberto urged. "We'd better get on with this, and be on our way."

"Roberto!" cautioned Meiying. "Why don't we introduce ourselves?"

Reluctantly, the woman gave them her own name. Valeriya.

"What is it that you're researching?" Viv asked her.

"I'm just a programmer," Valeriya said. "It's the computers that do the research. I'm only here to monitor, and perform maintenance."

"We'd like to take a look," Viv said, very politely.

Valeriya nodded, as though she had already weighed her options, which appeared to be few. "Please, come in."

The building had two levels; the living quarters were downstairs.

"On the second floor is our lab. There isn't much to see. We are mapping the human brain."

"You are scanning a new version of a human brain," Roberto corrected her.

"So you already know."

They didn't wait for Valeriya to lead them upstairs.

"Our test subject is not to be disturbed," she called after them, catching up with them on the landing.

They threw open the only door, and stared.

"This is our test subject, A-P-01," said the programmer.

"This is Sasha," Viv said at last. "This person's name is Sasha. And he doesn't belong to you."

"He's alive," said Enzi, standing over the body that was suspended in a frame, caught in a tangle of wires, tubes and cords. "We're taking him."

"He cannot be moved," protested Valeriya. "His skull has recently been opened. Why don't you wait for Semyon Mikhailovich? You only just got here. Rest a bit. I'll go and make some tea."

Ignoring her, they busied themselves disconnecting the electrodes taped to every inch of Sasha's bald head.

"What do all those tubes do?" Viv puzzled. "Roberto, please go and fetch what's her name. And we need the stretcher from the helicopter."

When Roberto returned, carrying the stretcher, his voice was alarmed. "Valeriya has locked herself in a room. I heard her talking fast. She must have some antique radio transmitter hidden away in there."

"All right, that's it." Enzi gave a few hard tugs at the tangle, picked up Sasha, and laid him, dangling wires and all, on the stretcher. "We're leaving."

It wasn't until they were outside, hurrying over to the helicopter, that Valeriya came running from the house.

"Semyon will not let you leave the country," she yelled after them. "You'll never get across the border."

Once they were in the air, Enzi grumbled, "She's right. Semyon has connections in the security apparatus. We won't get far."

"We won't have to," said Meiying. "I anticipated this."

So now it comes, Viv thought. *The hard part. The part were everything goes wrong. I never thought we'd even get this far.*

But the helicopter ride continued without incident, ending by a wide river, deserted but for one small freight ship. Its bow pointed in their direction. They waited until it had moored.

"Come on," urged Meiying. "Board! There's cabins for everybody. Make yourselves comfortable. It's going to be a ten day journey to our temporary home. Believe me, this will be the last place they'll come looking for us. Like Enzi said, Siberia is a good place to hide."

The freighter truly was more comfortable than it looked from the outside. But it wasn't the berth, or the bathtub, or the rocking motion that made Viv relax at last. Fiddling with an ancient computer in the control room, aimlessly going through her old internet stuff, she discovered an ordinary note. The message was from Stoker. He missed her.

So everything was going to be all right.

38

The Longstaff Institute of Artificial Intelligence, Nonamesset Island, Massachusetts.

The first thing Stoker noticed about the people he was meeting with: they were not dressed for a fight. Especially not a dirty one. A scientist, two guys who were supposed to be special agents, and an independent contractor—but none of them looked prepared to spill so much as a drop of ketchup on their starched shirts, pressed suits and polished shoes. Stoker was a careless dresser himself. He might wear socks belonging to two different pairs, one nylon, one bamboo, as long as they were the same color. Right now, in frayed cargo pants, scuffed sneaker-boots, and a faded tech shirt underneath a new twenty-six-pocket safari vest, he was ready for travel, for disaster, survival or attack, and for wherever Viv was.

"Mr. Quade," one of the agents addressed Stoker, shaking his hand formally, "Glad you could make it. Now, there's good news, and there's bad—"

Stoker raised his hand, fingers spread, as if to stop traffic.

"Good news?" he interrupted the suit. "You found her?"

They all exchanged quick looks that expressed absolutely nothing except that the bunch of them were insiders, and Stoker was an outsider. An outsider, and therefore a wild card. Gung-ho, desperate, not to be underestimated—what?

"Listen, Mr. Quade..."

"Stoker."

"Stoker, the message you received from the missing party was sent from a boat."

"A boat?"

"We were able to determine that it came from a moving vessel on a river in north-eastern Siberia. With the aid of satellite footage we were able to track its route to an isolated cabin on the arctic coast, where we believe passengers disembarked. This was three weeks ago, and we've kept the cabin under continuous observation."

"You mean they're still there? Viv is someplace in Russia?"

"We have reason to believe she is."

"So what's stopping us? Why didn't you tell me right away where I could find her?"

Stoker didn't like this 'good news—bad news' game. If there was news, he would decide for himself how to feel about it.

"Now, the bad news," insisted the agent, "is that Viv Caraway is wanted by the Russian police. She is effectively a fugitive. Moreover, she is still in Russia, and we can't simply walk in there with a team of commandos, and retrieve her."

"Oh, come on," said Stoker. "Russia is pretty much a failed state. We can do whatever we want. Nobody cares."

"It's not that simple. Miz Caraway is a person of interest for a Russian security agency, one of the more powerful ones."

"What do they want her for, anyway?"

Looks were exchanged once more.

"They claim Miz Caraway is part of an international gang that kidnapped a Russian subject from a Siberian research facility. The only reason why the Russians haven't gone after them yet, is that they don't know where the outlaws are."

The other agent took over. "We haven't told the Russians what we know, and the reason is that they are refusing to let American special forces conduct the extraction operation on Russian soil. So we made a deal. We will tell the Russian security service the gang's likely location, and in return, the Russians will release Viv into our custody. The way they capture her, though—that's not up to us."

Stoker sighed with relief. "So the others, Roberto and the whole lot, will remain in Russian hands? What would they hole up in that cabin for, anyway? Why haven't they moved on?"

"We assume they're lying low until the security services become less alert."

The contractor, who had been silently torturing his pen, leant over the conference table towards Stoker. "One more thing, Mr. Quade. You should know that the Russians are prepared to let you be present during their operation. They think you may be of value in potential negotiations. If you agree to go, I, as a non-government contractor, will be allowed to accompany you."

Stoker nodded, trying not to show how much this proposed role for himself pleased him. "Sounds good to me. When do we leave?"

One of the agents coughed. "There is one last thing we ought to discuss, Mr. Quade—Stoker. You could consider it a deal, a separate deal; this one between you and us."

For the first time the scientist opened his mouth. "The U.S. government will not press charges against Viv for any unlawful acts she may have committed here, or overseas. As her legal trulove you may take her wherever you want. First, however, we would like to do a thorough examination of her brain. We'd like to keep her under observation for as long as it takes, and determine, among other things, if her brain can still be considered...human."

"Fine," said Stoker. "Excellent. Whatever it is that they did to her head out there in Siberia, find out what it is. And then, please, undo it."

39

The northern coast of Siberia.

Sasha was the first to spot the visitors. He would be, wouldn't he? He spent more time outdoors than any of them, which was natural, after, as he put it, 'being stuck indoors' for so long. He liked to just stand there, at the arctic sea's edge.

In the past week, ice had started to form on the broad river mouth. How much longer should they stay? Sasha stared out over the gray openness of water and land, debating whether he should be feeling exposed or hidden. On the one hand, this 'hiding in plain sight' seemed madness. But the forgotten, forgettable aspect of the chilly landscape itself seemed to confirm what Meiying claimed —that this remote cabin, out of all the remote cabins in the world, was the most likely to be overlooked.

Also, hanging out in Russia a bit longer gave him the satisfaction of leaving his own country *in his own good time.* Surely, this was preferable to headlong flight.

"We will leave," Meiying had said, "as soon as I've figured out the safest place to take you. Somewhere ideal."

She came outside and walked over to him as though she already knew the question on his mind, but Sasha asked her anyway. "Are we expecting anybody, May?"

Meiying fixed her eyes on the distant plumes of dust and powdery snow that he had been looking at himself.

"An all-terrain vehicle," she stated. "Two occupants."

Meiying had good eyes. Her eyes were, Sasha believed, too good to be considered human any longer. The same was true for her hearing and her sense of smell. Her brain had found a way to improve on its sensory input. If a body can change a brain, she herself explained, why not the other way around? No one was all that surprised about those new, animal abilities of hers. It had often been observed, after all, that some human or other began to outwardly or inwardly resemble the animal he loved or cared for. And Meiying loved animals, she did—*all* animals.

"Men," she said, sniffing, and leaving her lips slightly parted, when the vehicle was closer.

From behind them came Viv's voice. "Don't worry. It's just Stoker."

They turned around. Viv held up her wrist. The tattoo was glowing.

"Eeee," she said, "How it tingles."

Stoker took Viv in his arms before she had been able to ask him anything. His embrace drew her back into another world. Sunday mornings, baking spice-bran muffins. Two separate minds full of mystery. Stoker, sailing his boat up and down the New England coast, hypnotizing her with his arm on the helm; letting ropes slide through his hands; tying knots. The shade of leafy trees. His irresistible physical possessiveness. Viv remembered normal life, and then, just as she was at her weakest, Stoker let go.

"You found me," she stammered.

"How *did* you find us? Enzi wanted to know. Everyone had come outside now.

Stoker grinned. "How could I *not* find you?"

"Love will find a way," said Roberto.

"Exactly."

"What about him?" Meiying gestured towards the Eroader, which had stayed behind at a distance.

"Don't worry about that guy. An American. A friend. I told him to wait by the vehicle."

"You're not staying?" asked Viv.

Stoker shook his head determinedly. "I've come to get you, Viv. Come home with me."

Viv said nothing. Her tongue lay in her mouth like a dead mollusk.

"You've achieved what you came for," said Stoker. "You helped your friend. It's done."

"Sasha still needs us," Viv answered. "All of us. He isn't safe here. And he hasn't fully recovered."

"Well, I need you too. And I'm warning you, Viv, this place isn't safe for any of you. You should get out now. Go get your stuff. I'll be waiting in the Eroader."

"How the devil *did* he find us?" Roberto repeated, once the five of them had retreated into the cabin.

Viv bit her lip. "Remember that time on the boat, when you asked me if I was thinking about Stoker, and I said I was? Well, to tell you the truth, I wasn't just thinking about him, I was talking to him. I happened upon a message, fooling around with the ship's navigation tablet. Still, I don't understand how he could have found out where we were, or where we were headed."

"I don't trust him," said Enzi. He paused, then added, "Something's coming."

Meiying nodded. "I sense it too. Something's wrong."

"What about our ride?" asked Viv.

"Our King Eider won't be able to get here for at least thirty six hours."

"What are you talking about?" protested Sasha. "What ride? Why should we have to get out of here so suddenly?"

"Thirty six hours," Roberto sighed. "If we can expect an attack, we may not last that long. We're sitting ducks here. We have no means of defending ourselves."

"Oh," said Enzi, "but we do."

With the words, "Give me a minute," he disappeared into a bedroom. But a minute went by, and he did not return.

Five minutes passed, and no Enzi. Viv and Roberto milled around by the small, splattered windows, now and then casting an anxious glance at the stationary vehicle outside. Meiying made tea. Sasha had stretched out on the couch by the gas stove, and all but fell asleep, as he usually did after a walk.

"What's taking Enzi...?" Meiying muttered at last, and Roberto grumbled, "I'll see if I can give him a hand."

From the far side of the room came a laugh—Enzi's rich, easy laugh, and yet, they didn't see the man. All they observed was that the doorstep, the floor behind, and the doorway were becoming unfocused. Outlines blurred as though the space itself were moving towards them. Then the green curtain became unfocused, the bookshelf, the rug, the gas stove. Following a path through the room, contours were briefly disturbed, as if by a slow wave, before returning to normal.

"I can see your eyes," Sasha said, sitting up. "And your mouth. Nose, ears."

"Oh my god," said Viv. "You were standing there all along? You're invisible?"

"That depends on your definition of invisible," said Enzi, winking at Roberto. "What does invisible mean but 'unseeable'? So, as long as no one sees me, I'm invisible. But if you think that you were looking right through me, then you're wrong."

Meiying drew her fingers over the place where they could vaguely see Enzi's arm, which had now taken on the shades of the cracked leather armchair he had seated himself in. "What is this you're wearing? It feels silky."

"I call it a cham suit," Enzi answered.

"A chemical suit?"

"Not chemical—cham for chameleon. The ultimate camouflage."

"Enzi, it's exactly what we need! Don't tell me you have only one of them."

"There's five," Enzi reassured Meiying. "They fold up very small."

"But how do they work?" Viv wanted to know.

"Later," Enzi answered. "There are other things we should discuss. Besides, I have a mind to never reveal how I made these. I think we shouldn't necessarily share all our recipes. That way, if any one of us is captured, the way Sasha was, they won't get *everything*."

Roberto coughed, airing some dissatisfaction. "So you're suggesting, if Stoker comes back and causes trouble, we simply hide?"

Enzi peeled a corner of thin fabric off his face, and stared back at Roberto. "We will conceal ourselves. And then, from within hiding, we will attack."

"You know, hiding doesn't sound like such a bad idea to me," Viv spoke up. "Just staying invisible, or badly visible, until they give up, is fine by me. Just fine! I'm not keen on the idea of shooting at people."

"Don't worry," said Enzi. "That's not what our defense will amount to. We will let the other side do all the shooting, bombing, burning, or whatever. All we need is these."

He opened a drawer, and from behind a box of chessmen pulled a small sack from which he took a little ball.

"I made thirty of these. Feel."

Sasha rolled the tiny wad between his fingers. It felt and looked a bit like crumpled aluminum foil, but finer, and more squeezable.

"That's right," Enzi surprised him by saying, "You're doing that right. Add some spit and continue. It's absorbing your DNA. Now—throw it."

Sasha obliged, tossing the wet lump across the room as casually as could be, but instead of landing in a waste basket or in some cleft between two pieces of furniture, the crumpled wad opened in mid-flight. The unfolding happened too fast for the eye to follow, and it only ended when the entire amount of material was spread out, stretched so thin that it could not really be called material any longer. It was a holographic image, not quite a spitting image, but still, a startling, life-size human shape with a rough likeness to Sasha. And it moved. It flitted and spun, brandishing some sort of gun.

"There's our defense," Enzi declared. "That's the counter attack. You'll see."

40

Stoker came walking towards the cabin, and the five of them went outside, but it wasn't to meet him. Their eyes were on the low, gray overcast through which nothing could be seen, even as an insistent, loud and rhythmic puttering announced a helicopter.

"Time is up," Stoker called out.

"Dammit Stoker," Viv snapped. "You led them to us."

"They're not here for you, honey. Just come with me."

"Forget it."

"Don't be an idiot." Stoker gestured at the swelling, deafening rattle and roar in the gray soup above their heads. "These guys do not come in peace. You have nowhere to hide."

"We'll take our chances. I'm staying. Goodbye, Stokes."

"Viv, what I did was for your own good. Using your message was my only chance to save you."

"Goodbye."

Stoker did not answer, turned away from them, and jogged back to the Eroader. He got in, but the vehicle didn't move.

The apprehension that had gripped the five friends when they went outside made way for an equally uniform determination. A sense of crisis overrode the individuality of their minds. They might have been born quintuplets, Viv thought, grinning. The others smiled and nodded, as if they knew just what had momentarily amused her.

Inside, they took off every last bit of clothing without the slightest self-consciousness. The cham-suits slid over their heads smoothly—loose, gauzy envelopes covering their bodies from head to toe, stretching easily as they spread their arms, but then, reacting with body heat, clinging to skin, hair and nails like melting nylon.

"Nowhere to hide, indeed," Roberto scoffed, as he watched the others fade and mesh with their surroundings, until the room seemed at the same time empty, and alive with blurry movement.

"And now?" asked Sasha.

"Each of us releases one spitball. Then we leave through the back door," commanded Enzi.

Sasha, lingering in the cabin for a few minutes, came out last, firmly shutting the door behind him. Once they had melted into the bleak background, Enzi laid out a strategy. Their dummies would lure the attackers to the house. Once the helicopter was unguarded, the five of them would take it, and make their escape.

They watched the helicopter land, and disgorge ten people from its black belly. Behind the smudged, un-curtained windows of the house, their virtual doubles, their 'spitting images', had begun moving to and fro. As expected, the visitors' attention was focused fully on the cabin. The ten men and women in body armor were clutching weapons; seemed on the verge of an assault— then stopped dead in their tracks. Stoker was running towards them, holding up both his hands, signaling 'Stop!' He spoke to them for a few seconds, then continued running, now headed for the cabin. The Russians stood down.

"Bad," said Enzi. "If Stoker goes inside, he'll see we're not actually there. He'll give away our game before we have the others clear of the chopper."

"It's me he wants," said Viv.

Not giving the others a chance to respond, she ran around the building, sprinting to meet Stoker before he got to the door. He did not notice her, of course; trotted on towards the front entrance. At last, Viv's thoughts caught up with her actions, and fell in with her heartbeat. *Change direction. Race to the sea. Stop. Turn around.*

She called with all her might. "Stoker!"

This time he stopped. He looked. Not at her; at the dummy image she'd cast ahead of her. Viv, too, stared after it. The Viv-thing seemed to have a momentum of its own, racing on, away from the house and away from the helicopter. But now it whirled around, pointing something.

"Wait!" Stoker screamed at it, running towards it. "Viv!"

"She's got a gun!" one of the men by the helicopter yelled.

He started following Stoker, who was nearing the dummy.

"Drop your weapon!" bellowed the Russian.

He aimed a rifle at the erratically darting phantom.

"Don't shoot!" Stoker screamed, even as a projectile wheezed past him.

Stoker spun around, standing in the way, raising his arms, and yelling, "Hold your fire!"—all in the few moments before the second shot. Stoker sank to his knees, clutching his right shoulder. No one else stopped moving. The Viv thing continued on to the wide river mouth. The Russian, obeying a command, rejoined his team, as it surrounded the cabin. The Eroader came powering towards Stoker. Stoker stood up, furiously mowing in the air with his left arm, motioning the driver on. The agile vehicle sped on in the direction of the river mouth. Viv saw her distant image lithely run onto the ice, and on, on towards the sea.

"Viv! To the helicopter! Now!" Enzi's voice came from nowhere, right nearby. "The others are already there."

"But what about Stoker?"

"His friend will come back and get him."

"I don't think he will. Look."

The ice was even less safe than the driver had had a right to assume, having seen it support a fleeing woman. Now, only the rear bumper of the Eroader was still sticking up above the river's surface, slinking from sight as they watched.

"He's lost. The Russians will help Stoker. We have to go."

"Sorry, pal, you can't come with us," Enzi, blending smoothly with the helicopter seats' upholstery, told the pilot.

Before the man's face had time to register surprise, it became immobilized, as Enzi pressed a tiny plug into the back of his neck. Hastily, Enzi and Roberto lowered the rigid body of the unconscious Russian to the ground and propped it up against a pack of gear.

"Wait a minute," said Viv. "Who's going to fly this thing?"

"I will," said Roberto.

"You know how to?"

"I know," confirmed Roberto. "We all know."

His tone was enough to make Viv realize that he hadn't ever applied the knowledge any more than she had.

As Roberto went through a checklist, the others kept their eyes on the cabin. One of the Russians yanked open the rickety wooden door, and threw something inside. Only Meiying's eyes were keen enough to register the spark. But everybody saw the explosion that followed, flinging the Russian attackers in all directions. Their temporary furnished home with all its virtual occupants spat apart like a star, leaving only a gulf of flames.

They looked at Sasha.

"Gas?" asked Meiying. "You tampered with the stove, didn't you?"

"It was us or them." Sasha shrugged. "We didn't come for them. They came for us. I'm not going to let them take me again."

The helicopter's engine was running. They put on headsets.

"But what if they're all dead?" Viv protested. "With the house gone, and no one left, what's to become of Stoker? He's wounded. Tonight he'll freeze to death."

"More Russians are surely on their way," said Enzi. "We've got to go. Roberto, take this thing up. Now."

Meiying, in the co-pilot's seat, punched coördinates into the flight system. "This way to a friendly cargo ship. If there's one place better still to hide than Siberia, it's the Pacific."

41

At first, only his heart grew cold. It was over with Viv. This was a feeling rather than a thought, an icepack in Stoker's chest. Then, cold was all around him, seeping into his fingers, his toes, spreading through his limbs, until every part of his body matched his frigid state of mind. Finally, Stoker began to see that coldness was, in fact, the essence of the world, of the universe, of God. He groped for memories, but each of them seemed a frozen-to-death piece of fantasy. He stopped walking. Why move, if there wasn't anything but cold? Why not sleep, right where he was? He let himself fall to the ground, satisfied with this simple way out, prepared not just to go to sleep, but to never wake up.

So this lady was Death. He had seen her before, though —that wavy hair, thick as night; eyes that sucked you in; the absentminded smile.

She felt his pulse, covered his body with hers. All the while, she was speaking, saying words he didn't understand. At last he caught sight of a handheld—she hadn't been talking to him.

"Nashla... Bystro... Zhiv..."

"I know you," he whispered.

"Hush. You are too cold. Help will be here." Her cheek rested against his. Her mouth blew warm breath into his ear.

"Sashura!"

"Yes. It's me."

But she was too young. Sashura was an old lady, middle aged; and yet, the body and face transferring heat into his felt as firm and smooth as Viv's.

"You're different."

"I've grown younger. A change for the better. Stoker. Wouldn't you like to change?"

"Change, how?"

She stroked his brow. "Change your mind. Expand it, the way your former friends have."

"They're no longer human."

"So what? Whatever they are, they're better than human. Superior. Think about it, Stoker. If you can't beat 'm, join 'm, what say?"

Stoker said nothing. The only thing he clearly understood, was that he was no longer cold and alone.

42

Somewhere in virtual reality.

Everything was just so. The retro futon couch with the scratchy mattress; the dirty mugs on the pine-and-steel cocktail table; the nineteenth century pictures of Mount Tom and Mount Holyoke; Stoker in his boat; and even the sprawling figure of somebody who had fallen asleep on the couch, with an open paperback upside down on his chest—he looked almost more like Stoker than Stoker himself ever had.

Viv turned around and around, tilting her face this way and that, to take everything in, and sighed. She was seemingly, *virtually*, in her old living room on Vernon Street. The only thing that was foreign, didn't belong here, seen from a nostalgic perspective, was a small oval mirror hanging by the door. She turned to it now, looked her image in the eyes, and said, "Home site complete. Save home site."

But she wasn't ready to return to reality quite yet. She bent over the sleeping three-dimensional Stoker, wondering if she could make it so that he'd wake up, open his eyes, sit up, see her, say something...

"Viv?" said a voice, not Stoker's voice, from somewhere impossibly far.

"Hey, Vivvi. Where are we?" Other voices now. She knew them all. They were in the room with her. She got up, turned away from the Stoker image, and there they were.

"Homesick, are you?" said Sasha.

"A replica of your home?" Roberto guessed.

"Hold on," said Viv, feeling caught. She looked in the oval mirror and commanded, "Flight Switch—Off."

In a perfectly timed overlap, reality began to shine through virtual reality. Clearer and brighter and more detailed it became, to the point where a very different setting had for 100 percent overtaken the illusory living room. They all blinked, staying exactly where they were, letting their eyes and minds adjust to the real world. The porch with the bamboo chairs and the glass walls overlooking the bay. Palm trees fringing miles and miles of yellow beach that lay waiting for them and them alone. A crinkling white line edging the blue ocean's immensity.

"Wow. That was so realistic," Meiying complimented Viv.

"Nice work, sister," said Enzi.

Sasha stood in front of the oval mirror by the door that led into the house—the only visual thing that had stayed the same through both worlds. He stared at reality's predictable reflection with fascination.

"Can't wait to try your *Flight Switch*."

"Thanks," said Viv. "It beats wearing a Fuga helmet, doesn't it? Still, it remains an escapist thing. A frivolous toy."

"That's what I thought when I invented the Springing Suit," said Roberto.

Sasha turned away from the mirror to face them.

"Virtual or real—escape is all we do. This life..." His arm wave encompassed house and view, "...it's terrific, but was this what Aquil and Shura had in mind when they got us together?"

They would have had a lot to say to this, but the room around them began, once again, to overlap with a different place.

"Wait a second," said Viv. "Who flicked on the Flight Switch?"

"Maybe you've got a hacker on your hands," Sasha suggested.

Viv tapped on the mirror, drew circles on it, blew on it —to no avail. The looking glass had gone to black screen mode, and the only effect of her manipulations was to produce a test image of a million colored, vertical stripes. Momentarily a human face replaced some of the meaningless output, but it was gone too fast to say for certain, let alone recognize who it was.

Meanwhile, the out of control visual process had changed the yellows, whites and blues of their porch's view into bone-white fog. Under their feet, instead of planks and rugs, now lay a cover of snow. The snow was blowing up in whirling, towering curtains. Viv could still faintly hear the others' voices through the roar of wind, but behind the dense snow drifts, none of them were any longer visible.

"Guys, are you seeing that?"

On the ground before her lay a man on his side. Powdery snow coated his body. Even before she crouched down beside him, she knew. How often hadn't she dreamed of him felled, wounded, abandoned?

"Stoker! Stokes, please wake up."

"Don't!" she heard the others shout. "Leave him. He isn't real!"

But she wiped the snow off his eyelids with her thumbs. Stoker opened his eyes, and looked straight at her.

"Hello Viv."

"You're alive!"

All the snow and fog, the whole white mirage melted away in less than a second. Stoker, however, was still present.

"I'm here," he answered.

"He's not real," Roberto repeated urgently. "Look at your wrist."

The truing tattoo was dark.

"Not real," Stoker confirmed. "Virtual."

"How did you find us?" Meiying wanted to know.

"Find you? I don't know where you are any more than you know my location. You may hide your bodies all you like, but not your minds."

"Stoker," said Viv. "I should never have left you there. We were running for our lives, you see?"

"For your lives? Do you really think those Russian forces would have killed you? They were firing tranquilizer shots. That's why I didn't get far, after I'd been hit. I fell asleep on the spot, and would have frozen to death..."

"Fine," said Viv, "Great! They'd have taken us alive and dissected our brains, and left us vegetables... But okay. Stoker, you couldn't know any of that. You were only trying to save me and do what you thought was right. Please, forgive me."

"Will you stop apologizing to that guy?" Enzi interrupted. "That isn't even Stoker. Can't be. Your boyfriend doesn't have the brains for any of this."

"That used to be true," said Stoker tolerantly, "but people change their minds, haha. I changed. Don't you get it? I followed in your footsteps. I have an A.I. implanted in my brain."

The five friends gasped as one.

"How is that possible?" asked Sasha. "Olimpio is gone."

"Olimpio wasn't the only one of his kind. That's all I'm going to say about it. And if you still doubt that I have all of Stoker's old knowledge, all his memories, just like you have kept those of Viv, Meiying, Sasha, Enzi and Roberto—let me remind you of a scene where all of us were present."

All eyes were on Stoker, but he had fallen silent. He raised his index finger, demanding their attention; then turned his head away from them, as though he were looking at something they couldn't see. But they *could* see it: something was there that hadn't been before. A veil, as yet, seemed to impede their vision. Fragments of a different room overlapped faintly with their own sunroom. A long dining table, and people seated at it, were projected onto their surroundings. The images grew in intensity, without ever fully supplanting the real world.

"That's Shura!" said Viv breathlessly. "That's us!"

At that point the dinner party memory acquired a soundtrack. The clear, past voice of Shura made Viv's own present voice sound thin.

"...Aquil thought he could change the way humans think," Shura was saying. "I think this is only possible if we change their brains. Our own brains. Imagine, for instance, adding Olimpio's intelligence to our own."

The earlier, virtual Roberto raised his glass with the words, "I drink to that. To Olly."

His fellow diners raised their own wineglasses, drank, shouted toasts of their own.

"Olly's innocence!" could be heard through the din.

"To the omnipotent Olimpio!"

"To A.I.'s impeccable manners!"

Finally, the lull, and that long-gone Viv putting down her glass, sounding suddenly thoughtful, "We would be gods. Well, demigods, at least."

"Roberto, god of flight!"

"I'd be the god of war. And peace, of course." That was Enzi.

"Goddess of animals." Yes, that was what Meiying had said.

The others looked at Viv, just like they had, and that past, ignorant version of Viv, how well she must have known herself, after all, offering smartly, "All right. How about Viviana, the goddess of health?"

Sasha followed, with his surprising, "God of power and authority."

"What about you, Stoker?" the giddy diners clamored. "Don't you want to be a god?" "What *would* you be the god of?"

Both virtual Stokers grinned, and the more transparent, earlier Stoker answered, "Let's see. What's left? Okay, I'll be the god of the planet Earth. *Someone* has to save the environment."

The veil-like scene faded, along with the voices. Their place and their selves were once again real and solid, except for the holographic Stoker.

"Very impressive, Stoker," said Roberto.

"Thank you. But I did not come here to impress you."

"Why *did* you come?" Sasha asked gruffly.

"I am here to propose we join forces. What were once dreams are now plans. More than plans. Deeds. You have all begun to tackle your pet problems and challenges. I will, too."

"That's good news indeed, Stoker," said Meiying with a face that did not betray any emotion. "So you want to do what's right for the planet."

"Absolutely. Thank you for getting to the point, May— what's right for the planet. So, what *is* best for the planet? Does it really take an upgraded brain to see it? Personally, I believe that if we didn't see it before, it's because we didn't *want* to see it."

"See what?" Viv felt her airways tighten.

"Simple. What's right for the planet is to remove what's wrong for the planet. Eliminate humankind. Let us, evolved beings, inherit an environment free of this pest called humanity."

"As far as I know, we are still human ourselves," objected Enzi.

"Not quite. You and I are no more homo sapiens than Adam and Eve were Neanderthals. We are a superior species. You must have come to the same conclusion. Our number will increase; our powers will grow; but it's impossible to change ten billion primitive humans into demigods. There's too many of them. And they do too much damage."

"We can't just murder all these people," Sasha protested.

"Murder," said Stoker. "Such a twisted human term. All those fine distinctions between various forms of killing. Did I not witness you trying to blow up ten of your countrymen?"

Sasha turned pale. "I couldn't risk letting them catch me again. Anyway, that was all the killing I ever intend to do."

"Enough," said Stoker. "Spare me further hypocrisy. Your faces speak for themselves. Clearly, our ways must part. I have my task cut out for me, and you have yours."

"Stoker," said Viv, "don't—"

Before she had finished her sentence, the handsome head with the sleek hair faded away. All that was left was reality.

End of Book One

About the Author

Hanna Wattendorff was born in The Netherlands in 1967.
She moved to the United States in 2001, and has lived
there ever since.
She is the author of *Ladies Without Servants and Other
Stories*, available from Amazon.
Visit Hanna's blogs at

relaxandreadastory.hannawattendorff.com
hunindie.hannawattendorff.com

Made in the USA
Middletown, DE
24 November 2021

53261635R00125